THE GUNSMITH

489

Town Tamers

THE GUNSMITH

489

Town Tamers

J.R. Roberts

SPEAKING VOLUMES, LLC
NAPLES, FLORIDA
2024

Town Tamers

ISBN 979-8-89022-165-0

Chapter One

Warbend, Montana

As Clint Adams rode into Warbend, Montana, he knew he would probably be there a while. He was detecting a slight hitch in his Tobiano's stride, and wanted to get it checked out. His intention had been to simply pass through town. Now those plans might have to be changed.

He noticed the strange looks he was getting from the people he rode past. Originally, he had thought of asking someone for the nearest livery, but these folks did not seem to be willing to help a stranger. Most of them studied him for a moment, and then quickly looked away.

He rode to the end of the main street before he came to a large livery stable. He dismounted and walked Toby to the doors. But before he could enter a large man appeared in the doorway, wiping his thick hands on a rag.

"There's something wrong with my horse's gait," Clint said.

"Take it somewhere else," the man said. "We don't treat your kind here."

"What do you mean, my kind?" Clint asked. "I just rode in."

The man studied him for a minute.

"You ain't with Elliston's men?"

"I don't even know who Elliston is."

The man frowned.

"You might be tellin' the truth."

"Look, my horse needs help."

The man's eyes flicked from Clint to Toby.

"Fine lookin' animal," he said. "Tobiano, ain't he?"

"That's right."

"Okay," the man said, "bring 'im in."

The man turned and went inside. Clint followed, leading Toby.

"Lemme have a look," the man said. "Where's the trouble?"

"Seems to be the left foreleg," Clint said.

"Easy boy." The big man leaned over, rubbed his hands up and down the leg, then lifted it from the ground. Toby wasn't happy, but stood his ground.

The man set the leg back down.

"Feels like a sprain," he said. "Not bad. I can work with it."

"What's your name?" Clint asked.

"They call me Bruiser," the man said.

"What's this about Elliston? Who's he?"

"He and his men came to town and took it over," Bruiser said. "They killed our sheriff and his deputy, and now they run Warbend. They've even taken some businesses, like a restaurant and a café."

"Looks like they've left you alone."

"They didn't in the beginning," Bruiser said, "but I lived up to my name, put a couple of them out of commission."

"And they left you alone after that?"

"So far. Elliston thinks he's gonna need me to see to their horses."

"But you told me you didn't serve their kind."

"I don't. Oh, they'll come after me sooner or later, but I'll deal with 'em then."

"Well," Clint said, "it better not be while my horse in here."

"Don't worry," Bruiser said. "I'll keep 'im safe. What's your name?"

"Clint Adams."

That seemed to shock Bruiser.

"What? The Gunsmith? You ain't here because of Elliston and his men?"

"I told you," Clint said. "I never heard of Elliston."

"Well look, our town council's looking for a way to get rid of him."

"What have they come up with, so far?"

"We ain't supposed to talk about it," Bruiser said.

"Are you on the council?"

"I am."

"Well, okay," Clint said. "If you don't want to talk about it, that's fine with me. I just want my horse taken care of."

"Don't worry," Bruiser said. "I'll take good care of him. I've got some liniment I cooked up myself."

"Good. Any idea how long it'll take?"

"I'll know more tomorrow," Bruiser said.

"All right," Clint said. "I'll get myself a hotel room."

"We have two hotels, but Elliston has taken over The Palace for him and his men."

"And the other one?"

"It's a small one called The Mayflower, owned by Patty Mayflower and her father."

"All right, then," Clint said. "I'll be at The Mayflower. I'll just need my saddlebags and rifle."

"I'll get 'em for you, and then I'll unsaddle your boy."

Bruiser removed the saddlebags and rifle from the saddle and handed them to Clint.

"Check back with me in the morning," Bruiser said. "I'll know more once I see how he reacts to the liniment overnight."

"Right."

"And try to stay away from Elliston and his men," Bruiser said. "One of them might recognize you."

"How many are there?" Clint asked.

"Elliston plus a dozen men," Bruiser said.

"Okay," Clint said, "I'll avoid them if I can, but I'm pretty hungry."

"Patty can take care of that, too," Bruiser said. "They have a small dining room, and she's a very good cook."

"Thanks, Bruiser," Clint said. "I'll see you in the morning."

When Clint walked out, Bruiser started unsaddling Toby.

Chapter Two

When Clint found The Mayflower Hotel he saw what Bruiser meant. It was small and clean, but would never be called the best hotel in any town. While clean, it needed some work. As he mounted the front porch, he had to avoid stepping on rotten boards, or his foot would have gone right through them.

As he entered the lobby he saw a difference between the inside and outside. The lobby was in perfect condition, with solid walls and floors, and a high ceiling. If the same care had been taken with the exterior, this would be a fine, albeit small, hotel.

As Clint approached the front desk a pretty, blonde young woman looked up from her work.

"Good afternoon, Sir. Can I help you?"

"Bruiser, over at the livery, told me this was the place to stay in town."

She studied him for a moment, her eyes falling on his gun.

"Are you one of Elliston's men?" she asked. "Your people are staying at the Palace Hotel."

"I'm not one the Elliston's men," Clint told her. "In fact, I never heard of him or his men until I got here."

"Then you're welcome here, Sir," she said, turning the registration book around.

"This is a pretty nice little hotel on the inside," Clint commented.

"Yes, we have some work to do outside," she admitted. "My father and I will get to it as soon as we have the money." Her pretty blue eyes hardened. "And as soon as we can get the town out from under Elliston and his men."

Clint signed his name, and left the space for his home blank, since he didn't have one.

The woman Clint assumed was Patty turned the book back around. Her eyes widened when she saw his name, but she didn't say anything.

"Here's your key, Mr. Adams," she said. "Room seven. Top of the stairs."

"Thank you."

"Welcome to Warbend, such as it is."

"Oh, Bruiser said I'd be able to get something to eat here. He told me you're a fine cook."

She smiled.

"I can have something ready for you in about twenty minutes."

"Thank you. I'll go upstairs and clean up.

In a small, clean, well-appointed room, Clint used the pitcher-and-basin to wash up, changed into a clean shirt and went back downstairs. He found Patty waiting behind the desk.

"Ah," she said, "Are you ready?"

"Ready, and hungry."

"Then come this way."

She led him into another room off the lobby. It had six tables and chairs set up.

"Have a seat," she said. "I'll bring your food right out."

"Thanks."

He sat at one of the tables to wait. When she came back she was carrying a steaming bowl of beef stew that she set down in front of him.

"It smells great," he said.

"How about some beer?"

"Yes, please."

"And I'll bring a basket of biscuits."

When she returned with the biscuits and beer she set them down and stood aside.

"Is everything all right, Mr. Adams?"

"This stew is wonderful," he said, "Miss . . . Mayflower?"

"Yes," she said, "but you can call me Patty."

"All right, Patty," he said. "And you call me Clint."

"I will, Clint."

She turned and left the dining room. Clint continued to eat. The biscuits were fluffy, and the beer cold.

He was finishing his meal when other diners began to enter. One by one men came in and sat, some alone, some in twos and threes. Before long there were ten men in the dining room, but none had ordered anything.

Patty came in and asked, "More beer, Clint?"

"Yes, thank you," Clint said. "Looks like you have a full house."

"Oh," Patty said, "they're not here to eat."

"Why are they here, then?"

"To see you, Clint."

Clint put his beer mug down.

"Me? What for?"

"As soon as my father gets here, he'll explain it to you."

"Explain what?"

"I can't—oh, here he is."

Another man entered the dining room. He was in his fifties, tall, with an impressive head of grey hair. He walked to Clint's table.

"Mr. Adams? I'm Henry Mayflower. I own this hotel, but I'm also the president of the town council."

"Ah," Clint said, "and these are the council members?"

"They are," Mayflower said, "and they're here because I called an emergency session."

"What for?"

"Why, to meet the Gunsmith," Mayflower said.

Chapter Three

"What's this all about?" Clint asked.

"Do you mind if I sit?" Mayflower asked.

"It's your place."

Mayflower sat.

Clint looked around and saw that all the men were watching them. Among them was Bruiser, from the livery. The others seemed to be businessmen in suits, and merchants in their work clothes.

"These men are all members of the council," Mayflower said. "I won't bother introducing each one."

"That's fine with me," Clint said. "I'm still waiting to hear what this emergency session is all about."

"You only arrived in town today," Mayflower said, "but already you've heard about Elliston and his men."

"I heard there's a man named Elliston who has used twelve men to take over your town."

"That's exactly right," Mayflower said. "The first day here they killed the sheriff and his deputy. They also took over the telegraph office so we can't send for help."

"Sounds like you're in a fix," Clint said. "What else have you tried?"

"We sent a rider out last week to try and find some help," Mayflower said. "We've heard something about a group called Bennigan's Rangers."

"I've heard of them," Clint said. "They're called town tamers. Sounds like what you need."

"I hope you're right," Mayflower said. "But until they get here we were hoping you could take some action."

"Me? What action could I take?"

"Well . . . you're the Gunsmith."

"That doesn't mean I can go up against twelve men."

Mayflower looked around at the other men, and then back at Clint.

"We're willing to pay you," he said.

"I think you better save your money for your town tamers," Clint said. "I'm just here to see to my horse."

"He's right," Bruiser said. "I have his animal in my place."

"It doesn't really matter why he's here," another man said, "he's here, and he's a gunman. We'll just offer him more money."

"Money's not going to do the trick," Clint said. "I don't hire my gun out that way."

"That's ridiculous," another man said. "He's a gunman, for Chrissake. Maybe he's here to work for Elliston."

"He never heard of Elliston until I mentioned him," Bruiser said.

"Are you sure of that?" another man asked.

"I'm sure."

The men of the council fell silent.

"I suppose that's it, then," Mayflower said.

"I think I'll go to my room, if it's all right with the council," Clint said.

"Of course, Mr. Adams, of course," Mayflower said.

Clint stood up, said, "Gentlemen," and left the dining room.

Mayflower sat back in his chair.

"So that's it?" Walter Sparks, the banker, said. "We have a famous gunman in town and we're not going to use him? What do we do when Elliston and his men decide they want the bank?"

"Let's hope that doesn't happen until Bennigan's town tamers get here," Mayflower said.

"You really think they're coming?" Sparks asked.

"I hope so."

"You sent young Charlie Perkins to find him," Sparks said. "You really think he's capable?"

"Charlie will get the job done," Mayflower said, standing. "You fellas can stay for some food. I'll send Patty back in."

Mayflower left, and half of the men followed, leaving Sparks and some of his supporters.

"Do you men know what I'm thinking?" Sparks asked.

"I think we knew you were thinking about Adams," one man said. "Suppose you tell us what it is?"

"I'm thinking if Elliston hears that the Gunsmith's in town, he might think Adams is after him."

"So you figure if Elliston hears that, he'll go after Adams."

"And somebody will kill somebody," Sparks said. "Hopefully Elliston will lose some men, or get killed himself."

"Or they might all just gun the Gunsmith down," somebody said.

"He's the Gunsmith," Sparks said. "He'd do some damage."

"So how do you expect to let Elliston know about Adams?" another man asked.

"I was thinking I'd go right up to him and tell him," Sparks said.

"And do you think he'll thank you?"

"I think he'll be interested," Sparks said. "I don't care if he thanks me."

"Well, all I can say is, I'm glad it'll be you, and not me."

Chapter Four

Well fed, Clint went to his room. He was hoping Bruiser would be able to get Toby on all four feet fairly quickly. He didn't want to be in Warbend any longer than he had to. And he had no desire to go against Elliston and his twelve men.

He assumed that Patty Mayflower had notified her father as soon as she realized who Clint was. And then her father called a session of the town council and told them. How long would it be before someone from the council decided to tell Elliston, thereby trying to pit him against the man.

He wondered if he should warn Mayflower not to try such a move?

At that moment there was a knock at his door.

"Who is it?"

"Patty Mayflower."

Still wearing his gun, he stepped to the door and opened it a crack.

"May I come in?" Patty asked.

He opened the door and stepped back. Patty entered the room quickly and closed the door.

"I didn't want anyone to see me coming in here," she said.

"What's on your mind?"

"I wanted to apologize for that ambush in the dining room."

"Oh, that. I assume it wasn't your idea."

"No, but I told my father you were here. That gave him the idea."

"Well, no harm done," Clint said. "They asked and I answered."

"They had no right to ask you to go up against a dozen men. You'd be killed."

"I guess they figured I might cut down the odds for the town tamers, when they arrive."

"If they get here."

"Right, if they get here."

"Have you heard of them, these town tamers?" she asked.

"I've heard stories about Captain Bennigan and his men," Clint said. "They've saved a lot of towns, but there have also been cases where they turned out to be worse."

"Worse than Elliston?"

"A bunch of men are a bunch of men," Clint said. "Give them the run of a town and something bad's going to happen."

"You think that'll happen here?"

"I think you and your people are just going to have to wait and find out what's worse, the sickness or the cure."

"I'll say good night, then," she said. "I'll see you in the morning."

"Yes, good night, Patty."

She left the room, and although it was early in the day Clint decided to just remain in his room. There was no point in taking a chance of encountering some of Elliston's men in a saloon. He would just stay in his room until morning, when he would go and check on his Tobiano in Bruiser's stable.

He had a couple of books in his saddlebag, so he decided to pick one out.

***

Walter Sparks entered the Panhandle Saloon and stopped when two men barred his path.

"Whataya want here?" one man asked.

"My name's Walter Sparks. I'd like to talk with Mr. Elliston."

"What about?"

"There's something important he should know about."

"You're the banker, right?"

"That's right."

"Wait here." He looked at the other man. "Stay with him."

"Right."

Sparks could see Elliston sitting alone at a table. The man who barred his way walked over and spoke with him, then returned.

"Come with me."

He led Sparks to Elliston's table.

"Okay, Denning. Leave Mr. Sparks here with me."

"Yes, sir."

As the man walked away Elliston said, "Have a seat, Mr. Sparks."

Sparks sat across from Elliston. The man was in his forties, wearing an expensive suit with a matching hat on the table.

"What's on your mind?" Elliston asked.

"There's something you ought to be aware of," Sparks said. "Clint Adams is in town."

"What? The Gunsmith?"

"That's right."

Elliston sat up straight.

"When?"

"Just a little while ago."

"What's he doin' here?"

"His horse went lame, or so he claims."

"Did your town council send for him?"

"Not us," Sparks said. "If someone did, I don't know who it was. But he's here."

"You spoke with him?"

"I did. He's at the Mayflower Hotel."

"Does he know about me and my men?"

"Yes, he does. Mayflower told him."

"Mayflower," Elliston said. "He's head of the council, right?"

"That's right."

"Then maybe he sent for him," Elliston said.

"Not without a vote from the council," Sparks said.

"And where is he now?"

"As far as I know, he's in his hotel room," Sparks said.

"All right," Elliston said, "thanks for the information."

"What will you do?"

"Right now, I'm gonna think about it," Elliston said. "You can go."

"But—"

"Just go, banker." Elliston waved Denning over. "Mr. Sparks is leavin'."

"Right this way," Denning said.

Given no choice, Sparks stood up and left the saloon. Denning returned to Elliston's table.

"What was that all about, boss?" he asked.
"The Gunsmith's in town."
That surprised Denning.
"What's he want?"
"That's what we're gonna find out."

Chapter Five

"How?" Denning asked.

"You're gonna go and ask Mr. Adams to come and see me," Elliston said.

"I am? Alone?"

"Take two men with you."

"When?"

"Tomorrow afternoon. In fact, ask him to come here and have lunch with me."

"Okay, boss."

Denning turned to walk away, but Elliston said, "Denning."

"Yes?"

"Take two men who don't look threatening," Elliston said. "I don't wanna spook him."

"Neither do I," Denning said. He went to the bar to choose two men.

Elliston gave the situation some thought. Adams might very well have been brought to town to go against him and his men, but even the Gunsmith wouldn't be that foolish. Twelve-to-one odds was just too much. But he still wanted to know why Adams was in Warbend, and the easiest way to find out seemed to be to ask him.

Doing it over food would cut down on the chance of gunplay.

***

It turned out it was much too early for Clint to simply stay in his room. He set aside the translation of the French novel *The Hunchback of Notre-Dame,* which he had only just started. He usually read late at night to get himself sleepy. But it was early evening and he was restless. And, despite the bowl of stew Patty Mayflower had made for him, he found himself hungry.

He decided to go down to the lobby and talk to whoever was behind the desk. As it turned out, it was Patty Mayflower.

"Hungry again, Clint?" she asked.

"How did you know?"

"I know men," she said. "That bowl of stew just took the edge off after you were on the trail. Now you're looking for a steak."

"Is that something you can rustle up, or should I go out and find someplace else?"

"No, no," she said, "I can do it. Besides, I don't want you running into any of Elliston's men."

"I'm sure your father feels different about that."

"Come and sit in the dining room," she said. "I'll get you a beer and then your steak."

"Thanks."

He followed her and sat at a table. She brought him a mug of beer, then turned to go to the kitchen.

"Will anyone else be in to eat?" he asked.

"I doubt it," she said. "At the moment we don't have any other guests."

"Is that because of the Palace Hotel?" he asked.

"The Palace was the best hotel in town," she said.

"Was?"

"Until Elliston and his men took it over," she said. "They've made a pigsty out of it."

"Then why aren't people staying here?"

"Word is getting out that Warbend is a gang hideout. People are bypassing not only us, but the whole town."

"Has anyone tried to get Federal help?"

"We had a telegraph, but Elliston and his men tore it down. The last telegraph we got said something about Bennigan's Rangers being nearby, so the council sent a rider out to find them."

"When was that?"

"Days ago," she said. "The rider was young Charlie Perkins."

"Young?"

"Fifteen."

"Why was he given such an important task? He's just a kid."

"The council didn't think the gang would stop a kid from riding out."

"Were they sure?" Clint asked. "They could have stopped him outside of town."

"Everybody's just hoping that Charlie got through," she said. "I'll get your steak."

He sipped his beer thoughtfully, and before long he could hear the sizzle of the steak in the pan and smell the meat cooking.

When she came out of the kitchen she was carrying a plate with a large steak on it, surrounded by potatoes and onions. She set it down in front of him and said, "Bon appétit. That's French for 'good appetite.'"

"I know," he said. "I'm reading a French book."

"You read French literature?" she asked.

"Well, it's a translation of Victor Hugo's Hunchback of Notre-Dame."

"I've heard of that, is it good?"

"Yeah, so far."

"Well, enjoy. We may have no guests, but I still have work to do. I'll check back with you."

"Thank you."

She went to the lobby, and he started eating.

Chapter Six

Henry Mayflower came into the lobby.

"You weren't here a minute ago," he said to Patty.

"I was in the kitchen. Mr. Adams wanted a steak, and since he's our only guest—"

"I get it," Henry said. "Is he in there now?"

"Yes, but let him eat. He'll be done in about fifteen minutes. I'll go in and get him some coffee, and then maybe you can join him."

"Good idea."

"Do you really think you might change his mind?" Patty asked.

"Probably not," Mayflower said, "but maybe he'll come up with an idea."

"Yes," Patty said, "maybe. How do the rest of the council feel?"

"I'm afraid they might do something stupid."

"Like what?"

"Somebody—probably Sparks—is dumb enough to go to Elliston and tell him about Adams."

"Then you have to warn Mr. Adams, Dad."

"Yes, yes I do," Mayflower said. "I'll do that."

"Let me see how far he is from finishing," she said, coming around the desk. "Wait here. I don't want him to feel like we bushwhacked him again."

She walked to the dining room, up to Clint's table. She saw he was almost finished.

"Can I get you anything else, Clint?" she asked.

"This was great, Patty. I wouldn't mind a piece of pie and some coffee."

"Coming up. Is apple all right?"

"Fine."

"My father usually has coffee and pie about now," she said. "Do you mind if he joins you?"

"Just him? Not the town council?"

"No, just him."

"Sure, why not?"

She went to the lobby to fetch her father then to the kitchen for the coffee and pie, bringing Clint's empty plate with her.

Mayflower sat across from Clint.

"Thanks for letting me join you," he said. "I'm sorry about what we did, but . . . well—"

"Forget it," Clint said. "You were trying to save your town. There's just no way I can do it, not alone."

"I understand that," Mayflower said.

Patty returned with two slices of pie and two cups of coffee.

"You're not having any?" Clint asked.

"No, I have work to do. You boys enjoy."

Patty went to the lobby.

"She seems to be a hard worker," Clint said.

"She is," Mayflower said. "She was going to turn this hotel around before Elliston and his men came to town. We're just lucky they chose the Palace as a sort of headquarters for their gang."

"Yes, Patty told me the damage they're doing over there," Clint said.

"Yeah, I feel sorry for Paul Gates, the owner. He had himself a gold mine, there. Now it's like a played-out mine."

"Patty also told me about this boy, Charlie Perkins, you sent out to find Bennigan."

"Charlie volunteered," Mayflower said. "And I know he did it to impress Patty. But we thought he had the best chance of riding out of town."

"They could've stopped him outside of town."

"I hope not," Mayflower said. "He's a brave boy."

"Sounds like a foolish boy, to me."

"That, too," Mayflower agreed.

Chapter Seven

"What do you plan to do?" Mayflower asked, as they finished their pie.

"In the morning I'll check with Bruiser on the condition of my horse. Then I'll make a decision from there."

"I have to warn you," Mayflower said, "I suspect someone from the council is going to talk to Elliston about you."

"And that wouldn't surprise me," Clint said. "There are enough men on your council that someone would come up with that idea. Who do suspect?"

"My guess would be Walter Sparks, our banker," Mayflower said. "He's dreading the day Elliston and his men walk into the bank."

"So it seems I'm likely to hear from Elliston at some point," Clint said.

"I'd say so," Mayflower agreed.

"Does he do his own gun work, or does he leave it to his men?"

"He wears a gun," Mayflower said, "it's silver-plated and he wears it in a shiny, black holster. The fact of the matter is, I've never seen him use it."

"He might be good enough to figure he doesn't need to prove it," Clint said. "Which saloon are he and his men in?"

"The Panhandle," Mayflower said. "They've taken it over. It doesn't serve anyone else. Are you planning on going there?"

"No," Clint said, "I'm just going to see if he comes to me."

"He'd probably send some of his men to fetch you."

"If he does, I'll go along," Clint said. "Right now I'm going back to my room."

Mayflower stood and said, "I'll say good night, then."

They walked to the lobby together, and Clint went up the stairs to his room.

***

The next morning Denning collected the two men he had chosen to take with him.

"Are we goin' against the Gunsmith?" Albie Hobbs asked.

"No," Denning said, "we're just gonna invite him to have lunch with the boss."

"Lunch? With the Gunsmith?"

"That's what the boss said."

"What makes him think Adams will accept?" the other man asked.

"He's just askin' him nicely," Denning said, "so nobody touches a gun."

"Don't worry," Hobbs said, "I ain't anxious to go up against the Gunsmith."

"Then let's go."

***

Clint spent a few hours reading, half expecting a knock on his door, but it never came. He figured if Elliston was going to send for him, it would be in the morning. He set his book aside, doused his light and went to sleep.

In the morning, he woke and went down to the dining room for breakfast. Patty was waiting for him and whipped up some flapjacks and a pot of coffee.

He was finishing up his breakfast when Patty came back in, looking concerned.

"What is it?" Clint asked.

"Three of Elliston's men are here looking for you," she said.

"Is that right? Well, don't keep them waiting. Bring them in."

"A-all right."

Patty went back to the lobby and returned with three men, all wearing guns.

"Are you Adams?" one asked.

"That's right," Clint said, without getting up. "What's your name?"

"I'm Denning," the man said. "I got a message for you from Mr. Elliston."

"What is it?"

"He'd like you to come to the Panhandle Saloon this afternoon and have lunch with him."

"What's he got on his mind?" Clint asked.

"He's the boss," Denning said. "He don't tell me what's on his mind. He just sent me—us—to invite you."

Clint looked at Denning, then at the other two men, who were standing by nervously.

"All right," Clint said, "tell your boss I said thanks for the invite. I'll be there at one."

"At one," Denning said. "I'll tell 'im."

Denning turned and said, "Come on, boys."

They walked out.

"Are you really going?" Patty asked. "To the Panhandle?"

"I've been invited," Clint said. "It would be rude to refuse."

"But he'll have all his men there."

"I think he just wants to talk," Clint said, standing up. "By the way, what is Elliston's first name?"

"Franklin, I think."

"Where's your father?"

"Probably in his office," she said.

"Can you take me there?"

"This way," she said, and he followed her.

Chapter Eight

"And you're gonna go?" Mayflower asked, when Clint told him of the invitation.

"Like I told Patty, it'd be rude of me to refuse."

"What if he just wants you there to gun you down?"

"I think he'll have some questions for me first," Clint said.

"I don't like it," Patty said, from beside her father's desk.

"I don't either," Mayflower said to his daughter, "but it's Clint's decision."

"But . . . somebody should go with him," Patty said.

"And who would that be, Patty?" Mayflower asked.

"I don't know."

"Don't worry about me, Patty," Clint said. "I'll be fine."

"When you get back," Mayflower said, "come and let me know what happened?"

"I will. I'll be in my room until I head over there about one," he said, and left the office.

After Clint left, Patty said, "You could go with him, Dad."

"I could," he said, "but I'm not brave enough."

She shook her head and left his office.

***

"Is he comin'?" Elliston asked Denning.

"He said he'd be here at one."

"Okay, then," Elliston said, "I want you and the boys out of here before then,"

"You gonna face 'im alone?"

"That's right."

"You think that's smart?" Denning asked.

"We're going to find out," Elliston said. "Meanwhile, you take the men to that other saloon, the High Card."

"They won't like it," Denning said. "So far we've laid off that place."

"Don't cause any trouble," Elliston said. "But don't take nothin' from nobody, either. Keep control of the boys, but do what you've got to do."

"Yes, Sir," Denning said.

"I want you to be out front when Adams gets here," Elliston said. "Just see him in, and then join the boys at the High Card."

"Yes, Sir."

As Denning walked away Elliston took his silver Colt from his holster and checked it.

***

At a quarter-to-one Clint came down to the lobby and saw Patty behind the desk. She hurried around to stand in front of him.

"I don't think you should go."

"I'll be back shortly, Patty. Elliston and I are just going to talk."

"I hope that's all," she said.

Clint left the hotel and walked to the livery stable to check on Toby.

"He's gonna need a few more days, at least," the hostler said.

"I want him to take all the time he needs, Bruiser," Clint said.

"Where are you headed now?" Bruiser asked.

"I'm having lunch with Elliston."

"I heard about that," Bruiser said. "Want me to come along?"

"I don't think so Bruiser, but thanks for the offer."

"Just be careful," Bruiser said. "Some of his boys are trigger happy."

"I'll keep that in mind."

***

Clint walked the several blocks to the Panhandle Saloon. He found Denning waiting for him in front.

"I'll take you inside," Denning said.

"Lead the way."

Denning entered the saloon, with Clint right behind him. There appeared to be only one man inside, sitting at a table. There wasn't even a bartender.

Denning led Clint to the man at the table, who stood up. Clint saw the silver-plated Colt in his holster.

"Adams, this is Franklin Elliston," Denning said.

"Mr. Adams." Elliston said, extending his hand. "Good to meet you."

Clint shook the man's hand.

"Have a seat," Elliston said. "That's all, Denning."

"Yes, Sir."

As Denning left Clint sat and looked around.

"No bartender?"

"He's in the back. He'll be bringing out our lunch. I want to thank you for accepting my invitation."

"And the rest of your men?"

"I sent them to another saloon," Elliston said. "Right now, it's just me and you, Mr. Adams. Just the two of us."

Chapter Nine

The bartender appeared with two plates, holding chicken sandwiches.

"We had chicken last night," Elliston said. "I hope you don't mind leftovers."

"This is fine."

"Coffee, beer or whiskey?" the barman asked.

"Coffee," Clint said.

"Beer for me," Elliston said.

The bartender went to the bar and returned with their drinks.

"That'll be all, Billy."

"Yes, Sir."

The sandwich was built high, stacked with lettuce and pickles and tomatoes. Apparently, Elliston's lunch invitation was serious."

Clint took a bite and found it satisfactory.

"Well, Mr. Elliston," Clint said, "suppose we get down to brass facts. Why'd you ask me here?"

"I heard you were in town, and you're probably hearing a lot of bad things about me and my men."

"You mean how you've taken over the town, and killed the local lawmen?"

"That sheriff and deputy came after us with guns blazing, Mr. Adams. What else were we supposed to do?"

"There's not usually an excuse for gunning down lawmen," Clint pointed out.

"Well, I admit my men and I make our own laws," Elliston said. "I was just wondering how long you were gonna be in town, and if we'd have to worry about you?'

"Worry about me?" Clint said.

"Yes, possibly being hired by the town council to come for us."

"Me against the twelve of you?" Clint asked. "That would take a lot of money, indeed. No, I'm just here until my horse's leg heals. I'd ask you and your men not to kill the hostler until my horse is better."

"I think we can promise that," Elliston said.

"Then I don't see that we have any potential problems, Mr. Elliston. Unless some of your men get it into their heads to try me."

"My orders are for them to stay away from you."

"And do they pretty much follow your orders?" Clint asked.

"Usually."

Clint sat back, leaving half the sandwich on the plate.

"Somethin' wrong with the sandwich?" Elliston asked.

"No offense but I'm still pretty full from breakfast."

"No offense taken."

"Then I'll say good day to you," Clint said, standing.

Elliston stood and touched the brim of his hat.

"Good day."

Clint hesitated.

"That's quite a fancy rig you have there," he said, indicating Elliston's holster and gun.

"I like to dress well," the man said. "That includes my gun."

"My tastes are pretty plain," Clint said, "except for my horses."

"A man with your reputation doesn't need to show off," Elliston said.

"Is that what you're doing with that rig?" Clint asked. "Showing off?"

"No, no," Elliston said. "I'm not a showoff. My gun stays in its holster unless it becomes necessary for me to draw it. And when I draw it, I use it."

"I'm the same way," Clint said.

"Then we have something in common," Elliston said.

"I guess we do," Clint said. "Have a good day."

"Have a pleasant stay in Warbend, Mr. Adams."

Clint nodded, turned and left the Panhandle Saloon.

***

After Clint Adams left, Elliston called the bartender over.

"Remove that half a sandwich, Billy, and then go over to the High Card and get me Denning."

"Right away, Sir."

Elliston finished his sandwich while he waited and went over his meeting with the Gunsmith. The man was very calm and collected, and walked into the saloon with no fear, even though he didn't know what he would find. He hoped nothing would happen to bring the Gunsmith after him. After their short meeting he found himself liking the man and would have hated to have to kill him.

***

Clint walked away from the Panhandle, finding himself impressed by Elliston. There was nothing threatening about the man, who was the leader of a large gang. As such, he probably kept a short rein on his men who, if they were smart, probably feared him.

Clint hoped it would never come to a head-to-head meeting between them.

Chapter Ten

When Clint returned to the hotel Patty gave him a look of relief.

"Thank God!" she said.

"Is your father still in his office?"

"Yes."

They both walked back to the office. Mayflower looked up from his desk as they entered.

"How did it go?" he asked.

"Fine. I had a good chicken sandwich."

"That was it?"

"He was alone when I got there, so it was just the two of us. We got acquainted."

"Where were his men?" Patty asked.

"He sent them off somewhere," Clint said. "He was very confident."

"He didn't threaten you?" she asked.

"Not at all," Clint said. "He was very pleasant."

"He can do that," Mayflower said, "come off that way, but he can turn quickly."

"Well, I don't think he'll have any reason to turn on me," Clint said.

"Hold that thought," Mayflower said.

"Why?" Clint asked.

"I've been authorized by the town council to offer you the job of sheriff."

"Thanks, but no thanks."

"Forty a month," Mayflower said. "You don't want to think about it?"

"No."

"Well," Mayflower said, "I told them I'd ask."

"What's the other saloon in town?" Clint asked.

"The High Card," Mayflower said.

"I think I'll go and have a beer," Clint said, "maybe pass some time playing poker."

"What happens if you run into some of Elliston's men?" Patty asked.

"He told me they've got standing orders to stay away from me."

"And you believe him?" she asked.

"Why not? What reason would he have to send them after me?" Clint asked.

"Who knows why Elliston does anything," Mayflower asked. "I'm waiting for him to get tired of this town and move on."

"That might happen."

***

When Denning walked into the Panhandle he joined Elliston at his table.

"How did it go, boss?" he asked.

"It was very pleasant," Elliston said. "He's a friendly fella."

"The Gunsmith?"

"A very calm man. I could tell he's as good as his reputation says he is."

"You gonna try him, boss?" Denning asked.

"There's no reason to," Elliston said. "He'll be gone as soon as his horse's leg heals. You make sure the men know I don't want any trouble with Adams."

Denning remained silent for a moment, then asked, "You ain't afraid of him, are ya, boss?"

"I respect him, Denning," Elliston said. "You and the men better do the same."

"There's already been some talk from a couple of them about tryin' him," Denning admitted.

"Who?"

"Baltimore Bob and Sam Weaver."

"Baltimore Bob?" Elliston repeated. "With a name like that?"

"I'll warn them off," Denning said.

"You know what?" Elliston said, "leave it as it is. If Adams kills Bob it's no loss. Maybe it'll be a good warning to the others. Meanwhile, go get 'em back here before there's trouble at the High Card."

"Right, boss."

Denning stood up and rushed from the Panhandle.

***

When Clint entered the High Card he could tell that most of the men there were part of Elliston's gang. They had taken over the bar and were being rambunctious. Other customers sat at tables, or rushed past Clint to get out.

Clint considered turning and leaving, but he really wanted a beer, and there was space at the far end of the bar, so he walked over there.

"Beer," he told the bartender.

"Comin' up."

When the bartender brought the beer over Clint said, "Rowdy bunch."

"Elliston's bunch," the bartender said. "They usually drink at the Panhandle."

"Looks like they drove some of your customers away."

"I figured they would," the man said. "You new in town?"

"I am."

"Well, I'd advise you to steer clear of them."

"Thanks for the advice."

"Bartender!" one of them yelled.

The bartender rolled his eyes and started to the other end of the bar.

Chapter Eleven

When Denning entered the High Card he saw Clint at the far end of the bar. He figured none of the men recognized him, or there would be trouble brewing.

He joined the Elliston men at the bar and said, "You men, the boss wants you back at the Panhandle."

"Good," one of the men said. "We got better beer over there."

The men scattered and started leaving the saloon. Two men looked at Denning and one asked, "So how did it go with Adams and the boss?"

"They got along, Bob," Denning said.

"Yeah? The boss ain't gonna try 'im?"

"He doesn't see any reason to," Denning said.

"Yeah, well, maybe we see a reason to, uh, Sam?"

He nudged Sam Weaver, who just nodded.

"Well," Denning said, "you might get the chance. He's standin' at the other end of the bar."

"He is?"

Weaver and Baltimore Bob turned and looked.

"That's him?" Bob asked.

"It is," Denning said.

"He don't look like much."

"He impressed the boss."

Baltimore Bob wore a derby hat and a vest over a dirty white shirt. Denning didn't think he looked like much, himself.

"Well, the boss wants all you men to steer clear, so let's go," Denning said.

"We wanna finish our beers," Bob said, holding up his half empty mug.

"Well, do that and get back to the Panhandle."

"Yeah, right."

As Denning left the saloon, Bob and Weaver turned to the bar and leaned on it, looking at Clint Adams.

"Whataya think?" Bob asked.

"Like you said, he don't look like much," Weaver said.

Bob looked around, saw that the saloon was mostly empty.

"Not much of an audience here," he said to his friend. "When we kill 'im we want a crowd."

"So we leave 'im alone?"

"For now," Bob said. "Come on."

They pushed away from the bar and left the High Card.

The bartender made a show of cleaning the mess Elliston's men had left behind.

"That was close," he said to Clint. "I thought those two were lookin' for trouble."

"Think your customers will start coming back in?" Clint asked.

"Yeah, they will."

"What are my chances of a poker game?" Clint asked.

"None."

"None?"

"Poker takes guts," the bartender said. "You won't find any guts in this town. Elliston and his gang have taken care of that."

"I see."

"You ever heard of them?"

"Only since I got here," Clint said.

"Well, they killed our two lawmen, and drove the mayor out of town."

"I heard about the lawmen, but not the mayor."

"Oh yeah, he packed up and left soon after Elliston and his men killed the law."

"Did Elliston have his men do it, or did he take part?" Clint asked.

"His men gunned down the deputy," the bartender said. "That brought the sheriff, Harve Benson, into it. He was a good man, been the law here for five years, but he had no chance against Elliston and that silver-plated Colt."

"Face-to-face?" Clint asked.

"Right in the street," the bartender said. "Harve never even cleared leather."

"That's a shame." Clint finished his beer. "Well, if I can't get a game up, there's no point in me hanging around."

"I got a couple of girls coming down in a while," the bartender said. "Come on back."

"Maybe I'll do that," Clint said.

He had seen the interest the two Elliston men had in him, and expected them to be waiting out front for him. He was satisfied to find the street empty. It seemed that Elliston's gang kept the street empty of any activity.

Passing the bank on the way back to the hotel, he thought of what Mayflower had said about the banker, Sparks, being the one who told Elliston that he was in town. He wondered if and when Elliston and his men would hit the bank. Most likely it would be on their way out of town. He wondered if Elliston intended to leave the town standing. Outlaw gangs like this one had a habit of burning towns to the ground when they were done with them.

Clint knew that thoughts like that had gotten him in trouble before. He hoped his Tobiano would be ready to travel before Elliston and his gang decided to finish with Warbend.

Chapter Twelve

The men were back in the Panhandle, including Baltimore Bob and Sam Weaver. Denning was sitting having a beer with Elliston.

"Some of the boys are wonderin' when we're gonna take the bank and burn the town down," he said.

"What's the hurry?" Elliston said. "They've got all the whiskey and tail they can handle, and the money in the bank's not going anywhere."

"You've got the best lookin' whore in town up in your room," Denning said.

"Yes, I do," Elliston said. "Thanks for reminding me." He stood up. "I'm going up and throw her a poke. Tell the boys they can go down to the whorehouse, if they stay out of trouble."

"Will do."

Elliston walked to the stairs that led up to the second floor. He had taken the largest room for himself and, like Denning said, he kept the best looking whore for himself, as well.

When he got to his door he opened it and stepped in. The girl on the bed lifted her head and looked at him.

"Hello, Daphne," he said. "Miss me?"

***

Denning watched his boss go up the stairs, then went to the bar.

"Any of you boys wanna go to the cathouse, the boss says it's okay. Just don't start no trouble."

"How long we gotta keep this up?" Baltimore Bob asked. "I'm lookin' to raise some hell."

"We raised plenty of hell when we got here," Denning reminded him. "Killed the sheriff and his deputy, drove the mayor and some other prominent citizens out of town. We take what we want from the mercantile."

"Yeah, but when do we hit the bank?" Bob asked.

"The boss'll let us know," Denning said. "Go to the whorehouse and raise some hell there. That's what those bitches get paid for."

"Only we don't pay 'em!" Sam Weaver said, and started laughing. "Let's go, boys."

Weaver left, with six men trailing behind him, including Baltimore Bob.

Bob was the one Denning was worried about. The boss was probably right. If he went after Adams, and the Gunsmith killed him, it was no loss.

But he didn't blame the men for wanting to raise some hell. He was itching for some hellraising, himself.

***

Elliston undressed slowly while Daphne watched. For an experienced whore, she was a good-looking woman. And she knew when not to talk, and just watch.

Once he was naked, he followed his jutting cock to the bed, and she knew what to do. She grabbed it, stroked it, then sat him on the bed, got to her knees in front of him, and gobbled it. She sucked him, avidly and wetly, the way she knew he liked it, then abruptly released his wet cock and jumped into his lap. She took his hard penis into her hot, wet pussy, and bounced on his lap, riding him like he was a bucking bronco.

And this was just the beginning.

***

When Clint got back to his hotel, he figured to just stay in his room and wait until suppertime. It wouldn't do for him to go out and find someplace else to eat. Patty was a helluva cook, and he was happy with all his meals, so far. And staying in the hotel would keep him from crossing paths with any of Elliston's men. He saw the one with the derby hat watching him, and if he knew that kind of man, he would be coming sooner or later.

He settled in with the Hunchback . . .

***

Elliston allowed Daphne to ride him for a long time before lifting her off of him and dumping her on the bed. He crawled onto the mattress with her, turned her over onto her stomach, then grabbed her hips and lifted her to her knees. She knew what was coming, so she lifted her butt high into the air and waited.

First he drove himself into her pussy to get himself nice and wet and slick, then withdrew, pressed the head of his cock to her asshole, and pushed. She gasped as he entered her and then began pounding away. It hurt like hell, but she went ahead and groaned aloud because she knew he liked it.

When Elliston had first chosen her and brought her to the Panhandle she thought it would be a good break from the whorehouse, where men grunted and groaned over her, and then rolled off and went to sleep. She also thought he would pay her well. What she didn't know was that he was as brutal as any of the cowhands who frequented the whorehouse, and he wasn't going to pay her one red cent . . .

Chapter Thirteen

Clint had supper with Patty and her father. She brought three plates out, laden with steak and vegetables, and then sat with them. She had also put a basket of warm biscuits in the center of the table.

"You must have been doing a pretty good business here before Elliston and his men got to town."

"Patty was raising our profile by the day," Mayflower said. "We were about to start work on the outside when Elliston and his men created havoc that drove people away. Now you're the only guest we've had in weeks."

"They've destroyed our business," Patty said. "Along with the town. Why are they staying around?"

"They'll stay as long as they have access to everything they want."

"If they keep it up, they're going to drain the General Store of everything it has, and Mr. Canfill can't restock."

"When that happens, they may decide to finish the job they started," Clint said.

"Finish it how?" Patty asked. "Won't they just leave?"

Clint remained silent, but Mayflower said, "Tell 'er."

"Tell me what?"

"Gangs like this don't just ride out when they've picked a town clean," Clint told her.

"What will they do?" she asked.

"They'll take whatever they can carry, which includes all the money in the bank—and then burn the town down."

"Burn it down?" she asked, appalled. "But . . . why?"

"That's what they do," Clint said.

"How do we stop them?" she asked, looking at Clint and her father.

"We don't," Mayflower said. "That's why they killed our lawmen."

"There are still plenty of men in town," she said. "Just arm them all."

"Elliston has twelve killers," Mayflower said. "We have shopkeepers and businessmen. If we had forty of them we'd still be outnumbered."

"You've got to hope your young Charlie found Bennigan and his men and they're on their way here. If they arrive—well, I was going to say everyone should stay off the street, but it looks like that's happening already."

"That's for sure," Mayflower said.

"All right, then," Clint said. "You'll just have to leave it to Bennigan and his men."

"And what if Elliston and his men are better?" Patty asked.

"Then nothing will stop them," Mayflower said.

The two men had been eating while they talked, but Patty seemed to have no appetite.

"Clint could do it," she said.

"What?" Mayflower asked.

"Clint could handle them," she said. "I know he can."

"Then you know more than I do, Patty," Clint said. "I've faced bad odds before, but not twelve-to-one."

"But after they face Bennigan and his men there won't be twelve," she reasoned. "They'll have to suffer some casualties."

"Fine," Clint said, "that'll bring the odds down to seven or eight-to-one."

"Still too much," Mayflower said.

Clint had wanted to stay out of the whole mess until his Tobiano was ready to leave town, but now he was getting to know these people. Patty and her father, and Bruiser, the hostler. He found he wasn't prepared to just ride out and leave them at Elliston's mercy.

"Maybe there's something we can do," he said, "while we wait for Bennigan and his men."

Patty's face suddenly brightened.

"You mean you'll help us, after all?" she asked.

"I won't wear a badge," Clint said. "But Patty had a good idea. There have got to be some men in town who will fight for their homes and businesses."

"Well, I'm no hand with a gun, but count me in," Mayflower said. "So that means there's two of us."

"Think it over tonight," Clint said, "and in the morning come up with a list of men we can approach."

"I can handle a gun," Patty said.

Clint looked at her and said, "It might come to that, Patty. It just might."

***

After supper Mayflower went to his room to give the matter some thought. Patty carried the plates to the kitchen and set about cleaning up. Clint went to his room, feeling sorry that he had chosen Warbend as a place to stop. Not that he had much choice in the matter. He couldn't have pushed his Tobiano much further, and the next town was over fifty miles away.

So he was stuck in Warbend, and while he was there he couldn't just sit and watch while Elliston and his men picked the town apart.

He was about to turn in when there was a knock at his door. He slipped his gun from his holster, which he had hung on the bedpost, and went to answer it.

Chapter Fourteen

"Who is it?"

"Patty."

It had to be her, or her father.

He opened the door and allowed her to enter, then closed it.

"Patty," he said, walking to the bedpost and holstering the gun, "what can I do for you?"

"You've agreed to help us," she said. "I wanted to thank you."

"You can thank me when it's over—if we're all still alive."

"That's just it," she said. "I want to thank you properly while we're still alive."

She started to unbutton her shirt.

"Patty—"

"Don't try to talk me out of this, Clint," she said, peeling the shirt off, revealing a frilly undergarment beneath it. She tossed the shirt aside, and began to undo her trousers. "I've been curious about this, so it would have happened at some time in the future. Only now we don't know how much of a future we have."

She sat on the bed to remove her boots, then slid out of her pants and frillies, and was naked. Fully naked, she stood. Her body was smooth and lean, with breasts like solid peaches.

"If you don't undress I'm going to feel silly."

"Well," he said, "we wouldn't want that."

She watched with interest as he undressed, and when he was naked she stared, wide-eyed. Clint closed the gap between them, took her into his arms and kissed her. Her mouth opened to his, and the kiss went on for a long time, while their hands roamed.

When he broke the kiss they were both breathless. As they moved to the bed, Clint found himself hoping her father never found out about this.

It had been some time since Clint had been with a woman this young. She had to be twenty-three or four. Her body was firm, her breasts and butt ripe. She had large, pink nipples that seemed to be begging for his mouth, they were so distended. He went to work on them, nibbling and biting while she writhed beneath him, then started to kiss his way down her body. When he pressed his face between her thighs, he found her wet and waiting. When he touched her with his tongue her body went taut and she groaned out loud.

"Oh God," she moaned, as he continued to work on her with his tongue and lips. He slid his hands beneath her butt to cup her cheeks and, suddenly, her body was wracked with waves of pleasure. She began to buck and he held her in place until she stopped. Then he mounted her and drove himself into her wet, steamy depths . . .

***

They laid together for some time after, catching their breath.

"That sure was a good way to say thank you," Clint said.

"I'd like to stay longer," she said, disentangling herself from his arms, "but I better get to my own room. My father might be looking for me."

"Well, we don't want him to find you here, that's for sure," Clint said.

Patty slid off the bed and started to get dressed. Clint watched every move with great pleasure. When she had straightened herself out and was ready to go she looked at him.

"Clint, what do you intend to do, now that you've decided to help us?"

"I don't rightly know, Patty," Clint said. "I found Elliston an easy man to talk to, so I guess I'll try that."

"You think you can talk him into leaving town?"

"I think I can try."

"I'd be amazed if that worked."

"To tell you the truth, so would I, but I'll try that before anything else."

She walked to the bed and kissed him goodnight.

"I'll see you in the morning for breakfast."

"Good night, Patty."

She turned and left the room.

Rather than remain naked, Clint pulled on his skivvies and then returned to the bed, which was still warm and fragrant from Patty.

He didn't know what tact he would take in talking to Elliston. The man seemed a reasonable sort. But he had already wreaked havoc on Warbend, including theft and murder. Could you really talk to a man like that? Maybe he could at least find out what the man's plans were for the near future. He certainly wasn't going to stay in town with his men forever. Not while there were other ripe towns out there to be picked.

He almost wished he hadn't stopped in Warbend for Toby to heal. He could have gone in another direction, to another town, and then he wouldn't know anything about what was happening in Warbend.

Now he had managed to get himself right in the middle of it.

Chapter Fifteen

Clint found Mayflower waiting for him the next morning in the dining room.

"Patty's getting breakfast ready," he told Clint. "Bacon-and-eggs."

"Sounds good," Clint said, as he sat. "How was your night?"

"Restless," Mayflower admitted. "I managed to come up with half a dozen names of men I think we can count on."

"That's it?" Clint asked.

"I told you," Mayflower said, "we're all storekeepers and businessmen. There's not a gun hand in town."

"What about outside of town?" Clint asked. "Are there ranches?"

"Yes, but they've all stopped coming to town. They're going elsewhere for supplies, and fun, so they can avoid Elliston and his men."

"You don't think you can get any men from outside?"

"Cowhands," Mayflower said. "No match for Elliston and his killers. If only our telegraph was working, we could send for help."

"Well, you did what you could by sending Charlie out. Unless there's someone else in town who wants to try."

"They're all afraid Elliston would blast them out of the saddle," Mayflower said. "What should we do now?"

"We've only got two things to do," Clint said. "We wait and see if Charlie got to Bennigan, and I go and have another talk with Elliston."

"What will you tell him?"

"I'll suggest that it would be a good idea for he and his men to move on."

"You'll threaten him?"

"No obvious threats," Clint said. "He wouldn't react well to that."

"You think he'll react better to something subtle?"

"I think we're just going to see what happens," Clint said.

"If you go to the Panhandle without an invite," Mayflower said, "all his men will be there."

"I realize that."

"You'd be taking a big chance without somebody to watch your back."

"I realize that, too," Clint said, "but I've gotten myself involved in this, now."

"All you did was ride into town," Mayflower said. "I wish Patty and I could have welcomed you in a better way."

Clint thought about his time in bed with Patty and said, "You've done just fine."

As Patty came out with their plates Mayflower asked, "When will you talk to him?"

"This afternoon," Clint said. "I might as well get it over with."

"You know he may send his men after you after that," Mayflower said.

"We'll have to see."

When Patty set their plates down Clint saw that he had a much healthier stack of bacon on his plate than her father did. He hoped Mayflower wouldn't notice.

***

As Elliston started in on his breakfast that morning he waved Denning over to his table.

"Sit down," he said.

Denning sat and remained silent.

"Have some coffee."

"Yes, boss." Denning poured himself a cup.

"What's the talk among the men?" Elliston asked.

"They're gettin' impatient," Denning admitted. "They're lookin' to raise some hell."

"And Baltimore Bob?"

"Definitely gettin' antsy, boss," Denning said. "He wants to try Adams."

"If he does, and Adams kills him," Elliston asked, "what effect do you think that'd have on the men?"

"Bob's kinda popular," Denning said. "I think some of the men would want to go after Adams."

"This might all be very interesting," Elliston said.

"Boss, when do you plan on taking the bank, and leavin' town?" Denning asked.

"Pretty soon," Elliston said. "I'm starting to get a little jittery myself. But I find this whole Gunsmith situation very interesting."

"You wanna try him yourself, boss?" Denning asked.

"You never know," Elliston said. He fell silent for a moment, then looked at Denning as if he wondered what he was doing there. "Okay, that's all."

"Yes, sir, boss," Denning said, and went back to the bar.

***

"What's on the boss's mind?" Baltimore Bob asked him.

"I ain't sure," Denning said. "He might be gettin' ready to call a play."

"I'm still lookin' to try the Gunsmith," Bob said.

"You know what, Bob?" Denning said. "I don't think the boys would mind that, at all."

Chapter Sixteen

Clint doubted that Franklin Elliston would allow his men to gun him down, en masse. He thought the man had too much confidence for that. If he wanted Clint dead, he would do it himself—or try. So Clint felt fairly safe walking into the Panhandle Saloon that afternoon.

Elliston was seated at the same table, concentrating on solitaire. He saw Denning standing at the bar with most of the men, including the one with the derby hat.

He didn't approach Elliston's table. Rather, he waited for Denning to notice him and walk over.

"What's on your mind, Adams?" the man asked.

"I'd like a meeting with Mr. Elliston," Clint said, "if he's available."

"I'll check."

Denning walked over to Elliston's table, exchanged a few words, and then came back.

"He's available," Denning said. "Go right over. Beer?"

"That sounds good."

Clint noticed all the men watching him as he strolled to Elliston's table.

"Have a seat, Mr. Adams," Elliston said. "I wasn't expecting you, today."

"I hope I'm not interrupting anything."

Elliston spread his hands over the table.

"As you can see, nothing vital. What can I do for you?"

Denning brought two mugs of beer over and set them down on the table.

"Thanks, Denning. That's all."

"Sure, boss."

Elliston took a gulp, set the mug down and asked, "What's on your mind?"

"Well, it appears I'm stuck in town until my horse heals," Clint said. "I'm hearing a lot of stories about you and your men."

"We did raise a little hell when we first got here," Elliston admitted.

"You call killing two lawmen raising a little hell?" Clint asked.

"They asked for it," Elliston said. "But by raising hell I mean we busted up some stores—and storekeepers— until they fell in line. Probably some whores, too."

"And what are your plans for the near future?" Clint asked.

"Why are you concerned?"

"Like I told you," Clint said, "I'm stuck here. If your boys start raising hell again, I don't think I can just stand by and watch."

"Are you taking over as the law, here?" Elliston asked.

"Not at all," Clint said, "but it seems I've already made some friends, and I can't just stand by if my friends are mistreated."

"What do you suggest, then?" Elliston asked.

"I think it'd be a good idea for you and your boys to move on," Clint said. "Find yourselves another town to bust up."

"So you don't mind if we have our way with another town," Elliston said, "just not this one."

"That's about the size of it, I guess," Clint said. "I can't defend every town, but I happen to be in this one."

Elliston laughed and said, "You're telling me this town ain't big enough for both of us."

"If that's how you want to take it."

Elliston waved his hand and said, "I've got twelve guns in here, Adams. One word from me and they all open fire."

"Well," Clint said, "that'd be too bad for me, but also for you."

"Me? Why?"

"Because before they can fill me full of lead, I'll put one slug in your forehead."

Elliston hesitated, then said, "Well, there's no reason for any of that, right now. You came here to try and talk me into leaving. I'm afraid we're not ready to do that, yet. Are you ready to stand alone against all of us?"

"No," Clint said, "that's not my plan."

"Then I guess we're done here," Elliston said. "Do you want Denning to walk you out?"

"I'm pretty sure I know the way, Elliston," Clint said, standing.

"Then I'm afraid the next time we see each other, we won't be so cordial."

"That's too bad," Clint said, and left the saloon, alert for any moves from the men at the bar.

After Clint left, Denning walked to Elliston's table."

"What was that about?"

"I'm afraid the Gunsmith has taken it into his mind to help this town."

"He's gonna stand against us?"

"He's going to do something," Elliston said. "We'll have to get rid of him before he does. Is Bob ready for this?"

"We just have to give him the word."

"Okay," Elliston said, "but don't let him go alone."

"Sam Weaver'll go with him, boss," Denning said. "Maybe the two of them can handle Adams."

"Let's find out."

Chapter Seventeen

When Clint reentered the hotel, Patty asked from behind the desk, "How did it go?"

"Not good. I think all I did was alert Elliston that I'm a danger."

"Will he send some of his men after you?"

"I'm counting on it."

"You want them to come after you?"

"He'll start slow," Clint said, "One, or two, maybe three. When that doesn't work he'll either send more, or come himself."

"And you'll kill him?"

"We'll see."

"What about Bennigan and his men?"

"If they get here, we'll leave it to them. Meanwhile, I think your father better call another emergency meeting of the town council. I want to talk to them."

"I'll tell him," she said. "What will you do in the meantime?"

"I'll be in my room," Clint said, "cleaning my guns."

***

Clint had finished cleaning his rifle, Peacemaker, and Colt New Line when there was a knock at the door.

"Who is it?"

"Patty."

He opened the door.

"The town council is downstairs."

"Good." He holstered his Peacemaker. "Let's go."

He followed Patty down to the dining room, where the council members were seated.

"All right," Mayflower said. "We're all here. Mr. Adams wants to talk to us."

"Why?" Sparks asked. "Has he decided to help us?"

"He has," Mayflower said, "even though you told Elliston he was in town."

"I was hoping it would scare him away," Sparks said.

"No one man is going to frighten Elliston," Clint said, "no matter who he is."

"Then why are we here?" Sparks asked.

"You need to arm some men," Clint said. "Mr. Mayflower says he knows of six who would do it, but you need more."

"You expect us to pick up guns and go against Elliston and his men?" another man asked.

"Not you," Clint said, "but there must be somebody in town who can handle a gun."

"Not to go against professional killers," Sparks said. "That's your job."

"I don't have a job here, Mr. Sparks," Clint said. "I'm offering my help."

"And we accept," Sparks said. "Now you get rid of them."

"You're being stupid, Sparks," Mayflower said. "You'd do better to just shut the hell up!"

Sparks looked offended, but fell silent.

Before anyone could say anything else, someone ran into the dining room. He looked to Clint like a young man.

"Charlie!" Patty shouted.

"I made it, Patty!" the boy answered. "Bennigan and his men are right behind me. They should be riding in any minute."

"Then let's go out and greet them!" Sparks yelled. He and the other council members rose and ran out of the room.

"Looks like you might be off the hook, Clint," Mayflower said. "Shall we go out?"

"We might as well."

***

One of Elliston's men was standing by the window.

"Hey, look!" he shouted.

The other men ran to the window. A few went to look out the door, including Denning.

"What's going on?" Elliston called out.

"Looks like about twelve men riding into town, boss," Denning said.

Elliston rose and walked to the batwing doors then stared over them.

"It looks like they're wearing badges," someone said.

"Federal marshals?" Denning asked, aloud.

"Let's not jump to conclusions," Elliston said. "Get some men with rifles at the windows upstairs."

"Right, boss," Denning said.

"What about Adams?" Baltimore Bob asked.

"He'll have to wait," Elliston said. "Let's see who these men are."

"Maybe we should run for it," somebody said.

Elliston turned and demanded, "Who said that?"

Nobody came forward.

"I don't want to hear that kind of talk again," Elliston said. "I want men upstairs with rifles, and men right here."

"You heard the boss!" Denning shouted. "Let's move."

***

When Clint and Mayflower got outside they saw the column of men coming up the street.

"Is that them?" Mayflower asked. "Is that Bennigan?"

"That's them, Mr. Mayflower," Charlie said. "Bennigan's Rangers."

Chapter Eighteen

The riders stopped in front of the Mayflower Hotel and one man dismounted. He looked at all the men gathered there.

"I assume this is the town council?" he asked.

"That's right," Mayflower said. "I'm the president."

"I'm Captain Bennigan." He was a tall man, in his fifties, with a granite jaw and slate grey eyes. On his chest was a badge that looked self-styled, nothing official.

"Shall we go inside?" Bennigan asked.

"What about your men?" Mayflower asked.

"They'll be fine out here," Bennigan said. "Let's talk."

"Very well," Mayflower said.

Sparks and the other council members began to move.

"Just you and me, Mr. Mayflower," Bennigan said. "My men will stay out here, and so can yours."

"As you say, Captain," Mayflower said. "The rest of you stay out here. In fact, go back to your businesses. I think everything will be all right now."

"But we—" Sparks started.

"Go back to your bank, Sparks," Mayflower said. "We'll talk later. Captain Bennigan? Shall we go inside?"

"What about Clint?" Patty asked.

Bennigan stopped and looked at her.

"Who's this lovely young lady?" the man asked.

"This is my daughter, Patty," Mayflower said.

"Did you have something to say, Miss?" Bennigan asked.

"Yes," she answered, "this is Clint Adams. He's been trying to help us."

"Adams?" Bennigan said, turning to look at Clint. "The Gunsmith?"

"That's right," Clint said.

"Are you involved in this matter?"

"I was just passing through town, but—"

"Why don't you come inside with us, if you have something to add?" Bennigan suggested.

"That's a good idea, Clint," Mayflower said. "Let's go to my office, the three of us."

Bennigan turned to his men and said, "Sergeant, keep the men right where they are until I come out."

"Yes, sir," the sergeant answered.

"Lead the way, Mr. Mayflower."

They went into the hotel and to Mayflower's office.

Patty stepped into the street and said, "I can get you men some coffee, if you like."

"That's all right, Miss," the sergeant said. "We've got our orders."

"Very well," she said, "but I'll get our dining room ready. You and your men must be hungry."

"Yes, Miss, we are," the man said. "Thank you."

She turned around and said, "Charlie, come inside and I'll feed you."

"Yes, Ma'am."

They went into the hotel together, while the other members of the council walked away.

***

When they got to Mayflower's office he said to Bennigan, "Would you like a drink?"

"I would," the man said, taking off his hat and wiping his brow, "we've been riding a while."

"I have some brandy," Mayflower said. "When we're done here, I can get you and your men some cold beer."

"That's fine."

Bennigan sat and Mayflower handed him a glass of brandy.

"Now suppose you fellas tell me what's been going on."

"Have you heard of Elliston. . ." Mayflower started.

***

"What's happening?" Elliston asked, from his table.

"The men are just sittin' on their horse, outside the Mayflower," Denning said, from the door.

"They're not doing anything?"

"They're sittin' there, boss," Denning said. "Whatta we do?"

"We wait," Elliston said. "We're ready for whatever happens."

"Yes, Sir."

***

When Mayflower was finished Bennigan sat forward and placed his empty glass on the table.

"They killed two lawmen?" he asked. "An official sheriff and deputy?"

"That's right," Mayflower said.

He looked at Clint.

"And you tried to get them to ride out?"

"I suggested it, yes."

"Did you threaten this Elliston?" Bennigan asked.

"Not exactly," Clint said, "but I made it clear I wouldn't just stand by and watch."

"Well," Bennigan said, "now that we're here that's probably what you should do." He looked at Mayflower, "Can you feed my men here? We'll do a better job if our stomachs aren't empty."

"My daughter can take care of all of you," Mayflower said. "And we have rooms for you."

"Good." Bennigan said. "We'll clean up and eat, and then deal with this problem of yours."

"We'll be very grateful," Mayflower said. "Let me show you all to your rooms. And we'll get your horses to our livery."

"Thank you." He turned to Clint. "I don't think we'll need your help, Mr. Adams."

"I'm still waiting for my horse's leg to heal," Clint said, "so I'll be around."

"Suit yourself. I'll go out and get my men."

He followed Mayflower from the room.

***

"They're dismounting, boss," Denning said.

"And doing what?"

"They're going inside," Denning told him, "and it looks like somebody's taking their horses to the livery."

"So they're staying," Elliston said. "We're going to have to deal with them."

Denning walked to Elliston's table.

"They're professionals, boss."

"Don't forget, Denning," Elliston said, "so are we."

Chapter Nineteen

When Bennigan and his men came down from their rooms, having cleaned up, they sat in the dining room. The easiest thing for Patty to cook was a huge pot of stew, which all the men seemed to appreciate.

Clint noticed that all the badges the men wore were crude, and he assumed Bennigan had them all made. There was nothing inscribed on them, they were just five pointed stars.

Bennigan sat and ate at a table by himself while the other men sat in three groups of four.

It seemed fairly certain that Bennigan did not want Clint's help, and he figured if they got the job done, that was fine with him. He thought it was going to come to a mass shoot-out between the two groups: Elliston's gang, and Bennigan's Rangers.

He didn't want to sit with them and eat, and thought that standing in the doorway and watching them was a bad idea, so he backed away, into the lobby. Mayflower was standing behind the desk, apparently at a loss for how to act. Clint walked over to the desk.

"I have to admit, I'm confused as to what I should do," Mayflower said.

"There's nothing for you to do," Clint said. "You have to leave it to Bennigan."

"There's something we didn't discuss," Mayflower said.

"What's that?"

"Bennigan's fee," Mayflower said. "I counted. He's got a dozen men. We have to pay them all."

"I'm sure you'll be paying Bennigan and he'll pay his men, but yeah, that's something you should nail down. And it's probably something Sparks, the banker, will have to be in on."

"He'll scream like a scalded cat," Mayflower said, with a smile.

"I'd like to see that," Clint said. "I think I'll go to the livery and check on my horse."

"I'll see you later."

Clint left the hotel, looked up and down the street before starting for the livery.

***

Denning was standing at the front window with a cold beer. He turned and called Baltimore Bob over.

"Adams is headin' for the livery," he said.

"You think I should take him while that crew is in town?" Bob asked.

"I don't think he'd be expectin' it. But take Weaver with you, just in case."

"Good idea," Bob said, and walked over to where Weaver was standing. The two exchanged some words, and then left the saloon.

***

When Clint entered the livery stable Bruiser was busy with the Bennigan Ranger's horses.

"Be with ya in a minute," he said.

"That's all right," Clint said. "You're busy. I'll check on my horse myself."

"I put him in a back stall, away from these animals," Bruiser said.

"Thanks."

Clint walked to the back and found the Tobiano standing comfortably.

"How you doing, big fella?" he asked. He stepped into the stall and ran his hands over the animal's sore leg. The Tobiano stood still for it. Clint could feel the heat from the liniment.

Bruiser appeared at the stall.

"He's healin' pretty good," the hostler said. "Maybe a couple of more days. But you might have something else to worry about."

"How's that?"

"There's two men outside the stable right now," Bruiser said. "One of them's got a derby hat."

"Two of Elliston's men," Clint said. "With Bennigan's Rangers in town I thought they'd be putting this off."

"The one with the derby is a mean one," Bruiser said. "They call him Baltimore Bob."

"Is that a fact?"

"You wanna go out the back?" Bruiser asked.

"No," Clint said, "somebody's trying to prove something. I might as well let 'em."

"I got a rifle—"

"Just stay inside, Bruiser," Clint said. "We'll talk about your rifle later."

Clint loosened his Peacemaker in his holster and strode toward the front entrance. Framed in the doorway he could see Baltimore Bob and one other man. Apparently, Bob thought he needed back-up.

Chapter Twenty

Clint stepped out of the livery stable and stopped.

"Baltimore Bob, isn't it?" he asked.

Bob looked surprised and pleased.

"You heard of me?" he asked.

"Not til five minutes ago," Clint said. "Before that I never heard of you."

Bob's face clouded over.

"That don't matter," he said. "Folks will hear of me after this."

"After what?" Clint asked. "You've got no witnesses."

"There's two of us here, with Weaver," Bob said, "and the hostler's watchin', ain't he?"

"Great, you have two witnesses," Clint said. "That'll sure get the word around. And does your boss know you're here?"

"The boss wants you gone," Bob said, "and I aim to oblige."

Clint wasn't sure if the man was going to act alone, or if the other man would draw with him. He had no choice but to watch both.

"Okay, then," Clint said, "the play's yours. Call it."

"This is gonna be a pleasure, Adams," Bob said. "Baltimore Bob guns the Gunsmith."

"You trying to talk me to death, Bob?" Clint asked. "You're doing a good job. If you can use your gun as well as your mouth, I guess I'm in trouble."

Bob grinned and said, "You don't know the half of it."

Bob went for his gun first, followed by Weaver. Neither man was good enough to outdraw Clint, who was immediately aware of that. He drew and shot Baltimore Bob in the chest, poking a neat hole in his leather vest. He followed that with putting a bullet dead-center in Weaver's forehead.

Both men went over backward, dead.

Bruiser came out of the stable.

"That was somethin'," he said. "And now Bennigan's group has two less to worry about."

"That's a good point," Clint said. "Where's the undertaker's place?"

"Don't worry about it," Bruiser said. "I'll drag them inside, and then go get him."

Clint ejected his spent shells, replaced them with the live rounds, and holstered his gun.

"I appreciate that," Clint said. "I better go and let Bennigan know he has two less to contend with."

He turned and started for the Mayflower Hotel.

***

"I suppose you expect me to thank you," Bennigan said, when Clint told him what happened.

"Not at all," Clint said.

"I told you we didn't need your help."

"I realize that," Clint said, "but they didn't leave me much choice."

"You could have found a way to back away," Bennigan said. "But wait, I forget, you're the Gunsmith. You don't back away from a fight."

"I do what I can to avoid fights," Clint said, "but this time I had no choice."

"Well, see if you can stay out of trouble the rest of the time me and my men are here."

"It'll be my pleasure," Clint said, and walked out of the dining room.

Sergeant Ezrah Sharkey came over and sat with Bennigan. He was a short, bowlegged man in his fifties who had been with Bennigan for years.

"Is he gonna be a problem, Cap'n?" Sharkey asked. "If he is, I can take care of 'im."

"I don't know, Sharkey," Bennigan said. "I guess we're just going to wait and see."

Chapter Twenty-One

In the lobby Patty came rushing up to Clint.

"Are you all right?" she asked. "I heard what you told Bennigan."

"I'm fine."

"You had to kill two of them?"

"Yes."

"That's good, isn't it?"

"Not according to Bennigan," Clint said. "He wants me to stay away from the action."

"You'd think he'd want help from someone like you."

"He has faith in himself and his men," Clint said. "And you hired him to do the job. I'm going to let them do it."

Patty turned and looked at her father, behind the desk.

"What do you say, Dad?"

"I agree with Clint," Mayflower said. "We should let Bennigan and his men do their job." Mayflower came around the desk. "I need to have another meeting with Bennigan to discuss price. And you better see if any of them want something else."

"Yes, Sir."

They both went into the dining room. Clint was at a loss as to what to do next. Then he made a quick decision. He was going to sit on the Mayflower's porch and watch the action. That was pretty much all Bennigan wanted him to do.

***

Mayflower took Bennigan to his office again, and the two men sat across the desk from each other. Bennigan had named a price, and Mayflower was stunned.

"That's a lot of money," he said.

"Half to me, and half to my men," Bennigan said. "That's the price."

"I'll have to talk to our banker, but I guess we can handle that. Of course, you get paid if you do the job."

"Of course," Bennigan said. "If we don't do the job, we'll be dead. You don't have to pay dead men."

"You have no families?"

"None of us do," Bennigan said. "I don't want any men in my command who would be worried about seeing their families."

"I understand."

Bennigan stood up.

"I'm going to talk with my men. Where are Elliston and his men?"

"Usually they're in the Panhandle Saloon. It's getting late. Will you wait til tomorrow to strike?"

"No," Bennigan said, "if we do, they might decide to strike first. We're going to make our move tonight."

"In the dark?"

"It's not dark yet, and it won't be for an hour. By that time they'll all be dead."

As Bennigan left the office, Mayflower hoped the man was right.

***

"What's going on?" Elliston asked Denning.

"Nothin' much, except—"

"Except what?"

"Well, Adams is sittin' on the porch."

"What's he doing?"

"Nothing," Denning said. "He's just . . . sitting."

"Did you send Baltimore Bob after him?"

"Yes, along with Sam Weaver."

"Then he must have killed both of them. Now he's just going to wait for those other men to do their job."

"But . . . who are they?"

"That's a good question," Elliston said, standing. "I think I'll find out."

"Where are you goin', boss?" Denning asked.

"Over to the Mayflower," Elliston said. "I want to know who we're dealing with."

"And what do we do?"

"Just wait," Elliston said. "If they kill me, you'll be in charge."

"Yes, Sir."

Elliston left the Panhandle and walked to the Mayflower.

***

Clint was surprised to see Franklin Elliston walking toward him.

"Don't get up, Mr. Adams," Elliston said. "I'm just here to find out who I'm dealing with."

"Go inside and find out," Clint said.

"If I go in there, they'll all probably gun me down. Come on, Adams. Give me a fighting chance."

"Is that what you gave me when you sent Baltimore Bob and the other man, Weaver, after me?"

"I knew you'd handle them," Elliston said. "They are dead, aren't they?"

"They are."

"Who are all those men?"

"I guess there's no harm in telling you," Clint said. "They're called Bennigan's Rangers."

"They're not law?"

"They wear badges, but they're not the law."

"Bennigan," Elliston repeated.

"Calls himself Captain Bennigan."

"I think I've heard of him," Elliston said. "What's your part going to be?"

"Me? They don't want any help from me, so I'm just going to watch."

"Do you know when they're making their play?"

"Not a clue."

"Would you tell me if you knew?"

"Probably not," Clint said.

Elliston smiled.

"Okay," he said, "I've learned enough."

"Then you better get out of here before they come out," Clint said.

"I think you're right," Elliston said. He tossed a salute at Clint, then turned and trotted back to the Panhandle.

Clint was very curious about which force of men would come out on top.

Chapter Twenty-Two

Bennigan sat in the dining room with his men and discussed strategy.

"They're in the Panhandle Saloon, across the way. They're bound to have guns in the windows. If we approach from the front they'll open fire."

"Unless we blast them first," Sergeant Sharkey said.

"Dynamite?" one of the other men asked.

"We've got plenty," Bennigan said. "A few bundles tossed through the windows, and then we rush in and finish them. Where's the dynamite, Sergeant?"

"In my saddlebags, Sir."

"In your room?"

"Yes, Sir."

"Get it."

"Right away."

He ran from the dining room.

***

Patty was standing behind the desk, and saw Sharkey run from the dining room and up the stairs. When he came back down in minutes, she saw the bundles of dynamite he was carrying. As he ran back into the dining room, she hurried to her father's office.

"Dad, they've got dynamite!"

"They're going to do their job, Patty. We have to stay out of their way."

"But . . . they could blow up the entire town."

"I doubt that," he said. "They know what they're doing. They're probably going to blow the Panhandle with Elliston and his men inside. That sounds like a good idea, to me."

"But Dad—"

"We're paying them a lot of money to get the job done," Mayflower said, cutting her off. "So we'll let them do it."

"Yes, Sir."

She left the office and returned to the lobby in time to see Bennigan and his men leaving.

***

Clint turned when he heard the men coming out the door, with Bennigan in the lead. They were all carrying rifles, except for two men who were carrying dynamite.

Bennigan looked at Clint, who said, "Dynamite?"

"It always works," the man said. he stepped into the street and the other men followed.

***

Elliston was back at his table when Denning called from the door, "Here they come!"

"Toward us?" Elliston asked.

"They're out of the hotel but gathered in front."

"Are our men in place?"

"Yes, Sir," Denning said. "All the upstairs windows, and down here."

"Get them ready to fire."

"Yes, Sir."

Denning ran to the stairs and up, shouting orders to the men. Elliston stepped to the batwing doors and looked out. He saw all of Bennigan's men, who seemed to be armed with rifles.

Denning came running back down.

"They're all ready, boss," he said.

"Then get yourself ready, too, Denning. As soon as they start to approach us, we open fire."

"As soon as they hear us firing upstairs, they'll start, too."

"Okay, then," Elliston said. "Get ready."

Chapter Twenty-Three

"They're going to start shooting as soon as we approach the saloon," Bennigan said to his men. "When Sharkey throws the dynamite, we all hit the deck. After the explosion we rush in. Got it?"

All the men nodded.

"Let's go," Bennigan said.

Holding their rifles ready, they all started across the street.

***

Clint watched as Bennigan's Rangers started for the Panhandle Saloon. Elliston's men began to fire. He watched as Sharkey ran forward, utilizing a zig-zag route, and tossed a bundle of dynamite through a Panhandle window. As it blew he threw a second one, this one higher, through a second floor window. Immediately, the other men ran forward, firing their weapons . . .

***

Elliston started firing along with his men. Immediately, he heard the men on the second floor firing. Then he saw a single man running forward, carrying something, and then throwing it.

"Dynamite!" he shouted. "Take cover."

He dove into a corner of the room, while Denning and the others took cover behind the bar. The dynamite exploded. Pieces of the bar scattered everywhere and when the second bundle exploded, the ceiling came down, the men from the second floor along with it.

***

Bennigan's men entered and began firing. Elliston's men had lost their weapons in the explosions, and were easy pickings. By the time Captain Bennigan himself walked in, the shooting was over.

"Sharkey!"

"Yes, Sir."

"Report."

"Like you said, Cap'n," Sharkey said. "The dynamite did the trick."

"All dead?"

"All the men we found are dead, Sir."

At that moment something moved in the corner of the room. As Bennigan watched, a man stood up from a pile of rubble, coughing and brushing himself off.

"Sir?" Sharkey said. "I can take 'im."

"Wait a minute, Sharkey," Bennigan said.

The man stopped and stared at Bennigan and his men.

"That wasn't exactly fair, you know," he said. "Dynamite?"

"You must be Elliston," Bennigan said.

"At your service . . . Captain Bennigan, is it?"

"That's right."

"Somebody told me something about your silver-plated pistol," Bennigan said. "I assume you know how to use it?"

"It's around here somewhere," Elliston said, looking around the rubble. "Ah, there it is." He started to pick it up, then stopped and asked, "May I?"

"Sure," Bennigan said, "go ahead and put it back in your holster."

Elliston picked up the weapon to clear it of debris and dust, then holstered it.

"I assume all my men are dead," he said.

"Every one of them," Bennigan said.

"So I guess I'm under arrest."

"No," Bennigan said. "We're not lawmen. We were hired to kill you and your men."

Elliston looked around at the dozen men who were holding guns on him.

"They're waiting for your order to fire," he said.

"I won't give that order," Bennigan said. "It wouldn't be right. I'll just have one man take you."

"And if I kill him?"

"Then another man, and so on, and so on."

"Well then," Elliston said, "why don't you just do it?"

"Why not?" Bennigan asked. "Is your arm okay?"

"It's fine.'

"Whenever you're ready, then."

"I've heard of you, you know," Elliston said. "After I gave it some thought, it came to me. Yeah, Bennigan's Rangers. But I never heard you were a gun hand."

"You have a chance then, don't you?"

"And if I outdraw you and kill you, they'll all gun me down."

"Don't worry, they won't."

"Why's that?"

"Because you won't outdraw me."

Elliston, still covered with dust, said, "I guess we'll see."

He drew his gun. Bennigan easily cleared leather first with his worn Colt and shot Elliston in the chest. The man fell over onto his back, amid all the debris.

"Check 'em, boys," Bennigan said. "I want to make sure they're all dead.

Chapter Twenty-Four

Captain Bennigan waited outside the Panhandle Saloon, lighting a cheroot. He always smoked one after a job. Eventually, Sergeant Sharkey came out.

"Well?" Bennigan asked,

"All dead, Sir."

"What's the condition of the saloon?"

"Bad," Sharkey said. "The bar's been destroyed, and the second floor is now on the first floor. There's no ceiling."

"All right," Bennigan said. "Let's bring the bodies out and see if there's an undertaker in town."

"Yes, Sir. Where will you be?"

Bennigan looked across the street at the Mayflower, where Clint Adams was still sitting.

"I'll be across the street."

***

Clint watched Bennigan and his Rangers take the Panhandle Saloon apart. After the explosion, when they all ran in, he assumed Elliston and his men had all been killed. When he saw Bennigan come out and light a cigar, he was sure of it. He watched as the sergeant came out and talked with Bennigan, who then started across the street toward him. He remained seated and waited.

***

When Bennigan reached Clint he said, "It's all over. Job done."

"You sure took that saloon apart," Clint said.

"It was the best way to go," Bennigan said. "They're all dead."

"And Elliston?"

"I killed him myself," Bennigan said. "That fancy silver gun didn't do him much good."

"So what now?" Clint asked.

"My men will clean out the bodies," Bennigan said. "Does this town have an undertaker?"

"I believe so, but you better talk to Mayflower. He's waiting to hear what happened."

"Yeah, I'll do that." He tossed his cheroot into the street and stepped up onto the porch, but before going in he said to Clint, "See? We didn't need your help."

"No, you didn't," Clint agreed.

Bennigan went inside.

***

Moments later Patty came out. She stood on the porch and looked across the street at the Panhandle, which was now on fire.

As Bennigan's men brought the bodies of Elliston and his men out, a volunteer fire brigade came down the street.

"You said Elliston and his men would burn the town down when they left. Maybe Bennigan and his men will do it."

"The brigade should be able to keep that fire from spreading," Clint said.

She hugged herself, as if she was cold.

"They kill all of them?" she asked.

"Seems like it," Clint said. "Bennigan's reporting to your father now."

"I don't like that man," she said. "He frightens me, even more than Elliston did."

"Well, I hope he can pay them off and get them to leave."

"They'll be here at least overnight," Clint said. "Your father will have to talk to the banker in the morning."

"Mr. Sparks won't be happy," she predicted.

"Why not? He wanted Elliston and his men gone. Now he's got it. All he has to do is pay the piper."

"Mr. Sparks hates opening his safe," Patty said.

"Well, it'll be up to your father to make sure he does," Clint said.

"I guess so."

Clint looked across the street at the pile of bodies that were stacked there.

"Looks like the fire brigade has the fire under control," Clint said.

"They usually use the brigade to move bodies to the undertaker," Patty said. "This time it's going to be a big job." She dropped her arms to her side. "I'm going back in. I suppose it's all over. Maybe things can go back to normal."

"Well, for that to happen you're going to need a new sheriff, deputy and mayor."

"I know," she said. "That's going to be a lot of work."

"What about your father?" Clint asked. "Would he take the position of mayor?"

"I doubt it," she said. "He never really wanted to be president of the town council."

"Well, right now he's the man who has to deal with Bennigan," Clint said.

"I hope he gets it done soon," she said, and went back inside.

Clint remained where he was and watched Bennigan's men and the fire brigade work on cleaning up the mess. It was dark by the time they finished, and Bennigan's men came walking over to the hotel, laughing and slapping each other on the back.

They mounted the porch, walked past Clint and entered the hotel lobby. The sergeant, Sharkey, was bringing up the rear. He stopped and looked at Clint.

"What'd you think?" he asked.

"It was a bit of overkill, since you asked."

"The Captain always chooses the best and fastest way to go," Sharkey said.

"Well, he did that," Clint agreed.

"He sure did."

Sharkey followed his men inside. Clint decided to go in, as well, and see what was going on.

No one was behind the desk. From the noise, all the men seemed to be in the dining room. Clint went to the door and saw that Patty was doing her best to get them all cold beers. Bennigan and Mayflower were nowhere in sight, so he assumed they were still in the office.

There was nothing for him to do but go to his room and stay out of the way. It was probably what he should have done from the beginning.

Chapter Twenty-Five

In the morning, when Clint came down, Mayflower and Patty were in the lobby. There was no sign of Bennigan or his crew.

"Where is everybody?" he asked.

"None of them have come down yet," Patty said. "They were up late last night, celebrating. They made a mess of the dining room."

Clint walked to the doorway and looked in. It appeared that all the tables and chairs had been broken into pieces.

He turned as Patty said, "They're as bad as Elliston's men were."

"Well, your Dad will just have to pay them off to get rid of them."

"The sooner, the better," she said. "I've got to get this place cleaned up."

"Can I help?"

"That's all right," she said. "Charlie's going to help me."

"Then I'm going to check on my horse and see if I can get out of this town."

"After Bennigan and his men leave, I wish you'd stay," she said.

"We'll see. By the way, where else could I get breakfast?"

"Just come back here. I'll be able to make you something," she said, "but I don't think I'll be feeding Bennigan and his men."

She went into the smashed up dining room, while Clint left the hotel.

***

"If you wanted to push him I guess you could leave today," Bruiser said, "But I'd rather keep him here a couple a more days."

"There's no real reason for me to push him," Clint said, "so I'll stay."

"What happened at the Panhandle last night?" Bruiser asked.

"Bennigan and his men dynamited the place, then went in and cleaned up."

"Elliston and his men?"

"All dead."

"So the job's done," Bruiser said. "They should be leavin'."

"When they get paid, yes," Clint said.

"With Sparks holdin' onto the money, that may take a while."

"He's going to have to give it up," Clint said. "Mayflower needs to pay those men."

"That's gonna be between Mayflower and Sparks," Bruiser said. "Those two are usually arguin'."

"Well, Bennigan and his men won't stand for not being paid," Clint said, heading for the door. "And they could be worse than the Elliston bunch was."

***

When Bennigan came down that morning he went right to Mayflower's office.

"Good morning," Mayflower said. "Your men had quite a night last night."

"Sorry about that," Bennigan said, "I'll see it doesn't happen again."

"Well, it looks like I'll have to take you out for breakfast, on the way to the bank."

"Suits me," Bennigan said. "I'm hungry."

"Then let's go," Mayflower said.

He took Bennigan to a café between the hotel and bank called The Peachtree.

"The food's pretty good here. They haven't had much business since Elliston and his men came to town, but maybe that'll change now."

They entered and there was only one man at a table. It was Sparks, the banker.

"Sparks, this is Captain Bennigan. Captain, our banker, Mr. Sparks."

"Glad to meet you," Bennigan said.

"You mind if we join you?" Mayflower asked.

"Not at all. I understand your men did the job last night, Captain."

"We made a bit of a mess, but the job's done," Bennigan said as they sat.

"And Elliston and his men?"

"All dead," Bennigan answered.

Sparks looked at Mayflower.

"We were coming to see you at the bank after breakfast," Mayflower said.

Sparks didn't look happy, and wanted to speak with Mayflower, but not in Bennigan's presence.

"Then let's enjoy our breakfast first," Sparks said, as a waiter came to the table.

Chapter Twenty-Six

When Clint entered the hotel lobby again, he looked into the dining room. Patty and Charlie were setting up tables and chairs.

"I thought all the furniture had been smashed," he said.

"We got these out of storage," Patty said. "Looks like I'll be able to serve breakfast, after all. And I'll start with you. Have a seat."

"Where's your Dad?"

"He took Captain Bennigan out for breakfast, and then they'll go to the bank."

Clint sat and wondered when Bennigan's men would start coming down. While he was sitting there young Charlie came walking over.

"Patty says you're the Gunsmith," the young man said.

"That's right."

"Mr. Adams, there's something I think you should know before those men come down."

"All right, Charlie," Clint said. "What is it?"

"The town I found Bennigan and his men in," Charlie said, "they picked it clean."

"What do you mean?"

"I didn't notice it until we were riding out, but it was like a ghost town. They took everything! So I rode on ahead to get here first, but I didn't have time to tell anybody until now."

"I see." Clint heard someone coming down from the second floor. "All right, Charlie," he said. "Don't mention that to anyone else."

"Yes, Sir."

As Charlie went into the kitchen, Sergeant Sharkey entered the dining room.

"Your boys had quite a time last night," Clint commented.

"I'm afraid that after a job they like to let off some steam," Sharkey said. "I'll see if I can keep them under control from here on in."

There was the sound of boots on the stairs and in the lobby. Sharkey turned as the men began to file into the dining room.

Patty appeared with a plate for Clint. She set it down in front of him, then turned.

"If you all take seats, I'll get breakfast for you. Ham-and-eggs okay for everyone?"

That was met with cheers and she hurried to the kitchen.

***

Clint ate his breakfast in the room with the loud men, and wondered if Sergeant Sharkey was actually going to keep control of them.

Patty, with Charlie's help, got all the men served, and the eating seemed to quiet them down, some. Also, all that was available for them to drink was coffee, so there was no drunkenness.

He finished his breakfast and carried his plate into the kitchen.

"I'm afraid they're going to start breaking furniture again," Patty said.

"The sergeant assured me he'll keep them under control," Clint told her. "Besides, they're not drunk. When they finish eating I think they'll just leave the hotel to look the town over."

"To look for more of Elliston's men?" she asked.

"No," he said, "I'm pretty sure they took care of all of them."

"Then what would they be looking for?" she asked.

He really didn't want to alarm her, but he replied, "Well, Charlie told me something . . ."

Chapter Twenty-Seven

When they finished their breakfast Mayflower and Sparks escorted Bennigan to the bank. Sparks used his key to unlock the front door.

"Do you have any employees?" Bennigan asked.

"A couple of tellers and a clerk," Sparks said. "They'll be here in half-an-hour. Now if you don't mind waiting out here, Mr. Bennigan and I will get your money."

"Suits me," Bennigan said. He walked to the window and stared out at the town as it woke up.

"Let's go into my office," Sparks said to Mayflower.

"But the money's in the safe, back here," Mayflower said, pointing behind the teller's cages.

"We need to talk."

Sparks went into his office and Mayflower followed.

"What's this all about?" Mayflower asked, as Sparks closed the door and locked it. Then he turned to face Mayflower.

"I'm not paying that man the amount of money you promised him.

"What are you talking about?" Mayflower asked. "They did the job we hired them to do. We have to pay them what we negotiated."

"I say renegotiate," Sparks said. "I can't take a crazy amount of money like that out of the safe. It's not just the town's money, it's our depositors."

"The whole town has to pay their share, Sparks. If we try to hold any of the money back, there's no telling what Bennigan and his men will do."

"They have to be reasonable," Sparks said.

"Who says?" Mayflower asked. "Now let's go to that safe and get the money loaded into bank bags."

"I want you to know I'm protesting strongly."

"Noted," Mayflower said.

They unlocked the office door.

***

"Are you serious?" Patty asked.

"If what Charlie says is true, these rangers could be worse than Elliston and his men. Your father has to get them paid and out of town as soon as possible."

"Does my father know what Charlie told you?"

"I don't think so," Clint said, "but he should be paying Bennigan right now."

"If Mr. Sparks goes along with him," Patty said. "He tends to think of all the money in the bank as his own."

"I think your father can handle a banker," Clint said.

"I hope you're right."

***

Sparks reluctantly opened the safe, turned and looked at Mayflower, who was holding a bank bag.

"Are you sure about this?" he asked.

"What's the hold-up back there?" Bennigan yelled.

"We'll be right out," Mayflower shouted back. "Come on, come on, let's get them paid and out of town so life can get back to normal."

Shaking his head, Sparks started loading cash into the bag, when it was filled Mayflower cinched it, then picked up another one.

"Let's try giving them one bag," Sparks suggested.

"We can't hold out on them, Sparks," Mayflower said. "Come on, keep loading."

Reluctantly, Sparks started loading cash into the second bag. When he finished Mayflower cinched the bag, then said, "Come on, take one."

They each carried a bag out to where Bennigan was waiting.

"Here's your fee, Captain," Mayflower said, handing him a bag.

"Wonderful." Bennigan tuned to Sparks, expecting the man to hand him the other bag. "Mr. Sparks?"

Reluctantly, Sparks handed the man his bag.

"Thank you," Bennigan said. "I'll take these back to your hotel. My men are waiting to get paid."

"And after you've paid them?" Mayflower asked. "Will you be leaving town?"

"Well, you never know," Bennigan said. "My men might like this town. Thank you, gentlemen."

Bennigan turned and left the bank.

"They're not going to leave town!" Sparks said. "What are we going to do?"

"Well," Mayflower said, "the first thing we have to do is hire ourselves a new sheriff, and elect a new mayor."

"What about Clint Adams for sheriff?"

"He's already turned the job down. We better have an emergency meeting of the council."

Sparks shook his head and lamented, "All that money."

"Never mind that," Mayflower said. "Come on."

Chapter Twenty-Eight

Clint was standing in the doorway of the hotel, waiting to see if any of Bennigan's men would return. What he saw was Bennigan himself returning, carrying two money bags.

As Bennigan mounted the porch Clint said, "I see you got paid."

"I did, indeed," Bennigan said. "Although the banker seemed very reluctant."

"I've heard that he has an unnatural attachment to the bank's money."

"Well," Bennigan said, "I better get these up to my room and start divvying it up."

"None of your men are here," Clint said. "They all went out after breakfast."

"I'm sure they're just looking the town over," Bennigan said. "They'll be back."

"Will you all be leaving after you dole out the money?" Clint asked.

"Everybody seems to want us to leave," Bennigan said. "We might like it here."

He went inside and up to his room.

When Clint entered the lobby Patty was behind the front desk.

"He got paid?" she asked.

"He did."

"And are they leaving town?"

"Apparently, not right away."

"Then when?"

"I don't know."

"If what Charlie said is true—"

"Let's not jump to conclusions. We'll just have to wait and see what happens."

***

There was an emergency meeting of the town council in City Hall. First things first, a member of the council named Daniel Lomax was appointed temporary mayor, until an election could be held. He was sixty years old and had lived in Warbend for thirty years.

"Next order of business," Mayflower said, "We need to find a new sheriff."

"Is this an emergency?" one of the members asked.

"Captain Bennigan and his men are not leaving town," Mayflower said. "I think we need a lawman as soon as possible."

"And how do we do that?" Sparks asked.

"Well, we need to get the telegraph back up, and send the word out to surrounding towns," Mayflower said.

"Is that what you want to do, Mayor Lomax?" Sparks asked.

"It seems to make sense."

"All right, then," Mayflower said, "we need some men to work on that telegraph. Let's get it done.

***

Mayflower returned to his hotel, found both Patty and Clint at the front desk.

"Dad," Patty said, "we need to talk."

"Come to my office," he said, and led the way.

When they got to his office he poured himself a brandy and sat at his desk.

"Okay," he said, "what's on your mind?"

"Tell him," Patty said to Clint.

Clint told Mayflower what Charlie had told him about the last town Bennigan and his men were in.

"Well," Mayflower said, "after we paid him, he did say he might not be leaving right away."

"So what do you intend to do?" Clint asked.

"We had an emergency meeting of the town council," Mayflower said. "We named a new mayor, and we're having the telegraph repaired. Once that's done were going to seek out a new sheriff."

"That takes time."

"Hopefully," Mayflower said, "we'll *have* some time."

"That will depend on what Bennigan and his men have planned for Warbend," Clint said.

***

It took two days to get the telegraph up and running, and a week to get a response from the call for a lawman. The new man rode in ten days after Bennigan's men killed Elliston and his men. He met with Mayflower and Mayor Lomax in the mayor's office.

"We're glad to have you here, Sheriff Temple."

Matt Temple shook hands with both men.

"I'm happy to be here," Temple said. He was in his forties and had a good record as a lawman for twenty years.

Mayflower handed the man his badge, and Temple pinned it to his shirt.

"Now tell me about Bennigan's Rangers," Temple said. "They're still here?"

"Still staying in my hotel," Mayflower said.

"Are they causing any trouble?"

"It's nothing like when Elliston and his men were here," Mayflower said. "They took over a hotel, a saloon, took what they wanted when they wanted it from the general store and other places."

"And Bennigan's men?"

"For the most part, they've been behaving," Mayflower said.

"What else should I know?" Temple asked. "I hear the Gunsmith was in town."

"He was," Mayflower said. "His horse was lame, but the leg healed, and Adams left a week ago."

"That's good," Temple said. "I won't have to deal with him." He got to his feet. "Forty a month, right?"

"That's right."

If you'll show me where my office is, I'll start interviewing deputies. Oh, and I'll need a place to live."

"We have a house for you on the edge of town," Mayflower said. "If you'll wait for me downstairs, I'll show you to your office."

When Temple left Lomax asked, "What do you think?"

"I think he'll do the job."

"And Bennigan and his men?"

"They haven't caused any real trouble, aside from some drunken nights in a saloon. He can handle that."

"I hope we're right," Lomax said.

Chapter Twenty-Nine

Clint spent one more night with Patty before leaving Warbend. He left there without ever having met Sheriff Temple.

As for Bennigan and his men, they were still in town. Repairs were being made to the Panhandle Saloon, so they did their drinking in a place called The Lucky Seven. They also visited the whorehouse, the general store, and some cafes, but had caused no trouble.

As Clint rode out of town, he hoped things would remain that way.

***

Sheriff Temple hired two young men, men he thought he could shape into fine deputies. One night, two weeks after Clint had left, the two deputies returned from their rounds.

"How are things out there?" Temple asked.

"North end of town's quiet, Sheriff," Deputy Mickey Tyler said.

"South end's a little loud," Lou Campbell said. "Bennigan's men are in the Lucky Seven again, and they're drinkin' hard."

"When are they gonna leave town, Sheriff?" Tyler asked.

"There's no tellin, Mickey," Temple said, "but so far they're staying within the word of the law."

"Have you talked to Bennigan, Sheriff?" Campbell asked.

"I introduced myself," Temple said, "but that was the extent of it."

"Well, it looks like Bennigan himself stays in his room most of the time, while his men are in the saloon, whorehouse and restaurants."

"Have they busted any of those places up?" Temple asked.

"A couple of whores got roughed up, and one waiter, but that's about it," Campbell said.

"What about the Lucky Seven?" Temple asked.

"No real damage," Campbell said.

"So things are okay, for now," Temple said. "Tyler you go home and come back in the morning," Temple said. "Campbell, you're on night duty."

"Yessir," they both said.

"I'm gonna go get some supper," Temple said, standing up and grabbing his hat. He looked at Campbell. "When I get back you can go get yours."

"Yessir," Campbell said.

Tyler and Temple left the office together.

"Where are you gonna eat, Sheriff?" Tyler asked.

"The Mayflower. They make a good steak."

"And Patty's very pretty," Tyler said.

"Yes, she is. And Bennigan eats there. I like keeping an eye on him."

"You want some company?"

"No, I'm okay," Temple said. "You go and eat where you usually do."

"I like the Peachtree."

"That's a good place." He slapped the young man on the back. "I'll see you tomorrow."

"'night, Sheriff."

Deputy Tyler turned and walked off. Sheriff Temple went the other way, toward the Mayflower Hotel.

***

In the Mayflower, Bennigan was coming down to the dining room for his supper. He also thought Patty was pretty and was determined to win her over by not treating her like a whore.

126

Chapter Thirty

Patty greeted Bennigan at the entrance to the dining room. Every so often he would be eating with one of his men, but not tonight. That suited her, because his men were crude.

"Eating alone tonight, Captain?" she asked.

"Only if you won't eat with me," he said.

"Now if I did that, who would cook?" she asked.

She led him to a table and he sat.

"A steak?" she asked.

"What else?"

"I'll bring you a beer to start."

"Thank you."

She went to the kitchen for the beer and when she brought it out, she saw Sheriff Temple coming in.

"There you go," she said, setting the beer down. "Excuse me."

He picked up his beer and turned to watch her walk to the door to greet the sheriff.

"Good evening, Miss Mayflower."

"Come this way," she said.

There were only half-a-dozen tables, but she seated the lawman as far from Bennigan as she could.

"Thank you," he said, seating himself.

"A steak, Sheriff?" she asked.

"Please."

"Coming up."

She went to the kitchen to prepare two steak suppers.

"She makes a good steak, doesn't she?" Bennigan said.

"She does, indeed," Temple said.

"You know, we've eaten in here at the same time before," Bennigan said, "but never together. Why don't you join me?"

"Why not?"

Temple stood up to walk to Bennigan's table, and Patty appeared carrying a beer for him.

"I'm joining Captain Bennigan, Miss Mayflower," he said.

"As you wish," she said.

As he sat across from Bennigan, she set his beer down.

"I'll be right back with your meals."

She returned to the kitchen.

"How do you like the job, so far?" Bennigan asked.

"I like it fine," Temple said. "The folks here are real nice."

"Are they?" Bennigan said. "They look at me and my men in a funny way. Like they're waiting for us to . . . well, go crazy."

"I'm sure they're still remembering what Elliston and his men did."

"And we took care of them," Bennigan said. "They should be looking at us like heroes. Instead, they hired you to watch us."

"They hired me to keep the peace," Temple said. "I watch everyone."

"You know, I've been keeping my boys in check," Bennigan said, "but they're gettin' a bit squirrely."

"They've been behaving themselves, for the most part," Temple said.

"Yes, they have," Bennigan said. "They're waiting for a signal from me."

"A signal you intend to give them?"

"Eventually," Bennigan said, "but not for a while, yet." Patty appeared with their steaks. "At least not until we've eaten."

She set their plates down in front of them. Temple studied Bennigan, wondering why he was telling him all this.

"Are you telling me your men are waiting for a signal to do . . . what?"

Bennigan began cutting his steak.

"The bank will be first," Bennigan said.

"But you got paid."

"Yes, we did," Bennigan said, "but there's still money in the bank. We can't ride away and just leave it there."

"So you're telling me you're going to rob the bank?" Temple asked.

"That'll just be the start," Bennigan said. "Eat your steak, Sheriff."

Temple picked up his knife and fork.

"What's next?"

"I haven't worked it all out yet," Bennigan said. He popped a hunk of steak into his mouth and began chewing.

"Why are you telling me this now?" Temple asked, cutting his own meat.

"Well, you and your deputies will have to stop us," Bennigan said. "I just want to give you a fair chance."

"So this is some kind of game to you?" Sheriff Temple asked.

"It's all a game, Sheriff," Bennigan said. "You've worn a badge long enough to know that." Bennigan speared a potato. "Go ahead, eat your supper, Sheriff. Miss Mayflower's cooking is too good to waste."

Captain Bennigan was right about that, so Temple started eating.

Chapter Thirty-One

Sheriff Temple left the Mayflower, wondering just what Bennigan's intentions were that evening. Was he serious about robbing the bank and the town, knowing that Temple would have to try and stop them?

Bennigan had a dozen men, while Temple had two deputies. Those odds were not good. But if Temple could take Bennigan out of the play, what would his men do, then?

He went back to his office, determined to figure out a strategy.

***

Patty had watched the two men eat, wondering what was going on. She could feel the tension in the air between them, and yet they continued to eat. When they were done Temple left the hotel, and Bennigan returned to his room.

After she had cleared the plates away, she went to her father's office. She slumped into the chair across from him.

He stopped what he was doing and asked, "What's wrong?"

"I just served supper to Captain Bennigan and Sheriff Temple."

"So?" he asked. "They have to eat."

"They ate together," she said.

That interested him.

"At the same table?"

"Oh, yes."

"And?"

"There was a lot of tension."

"Did you hear what they were talking about?" he asked.

"No, I couldn't hear them, but Captain Bennigan did most of the talking."

Mayflower sat back in his chair.

"It's been quiet, and I was hoping that was because Temple was doing his job."

"And now?"

Bennigan could be keeping his men under control, but why are they staying in town?"

"Maybe they're just waiting for another job," Patty suggested.

"I hope you're right," Mayflower said, "but as long as they're still here, I'll be waiting for the other boot to drop."

"Maybe Charlie was wrong," she said.

"We can hope."

She stood up.

"When's the next mayoral election?"

"Not for a few months," he said. "So far Mayor Lomax is going along with the council's suggestions."

"And Mr. Sparks?"

"He's hired his own security for the bank," Mayflower said. "Two burly types with shotguns. I don't know how good they would do in a real fight."

"I wish Clint was still here."

"He was determined to stay out of it, Patty," Mayflower reminded her.

"But he did kill two of Elliston's men, and before Bennigan and his men arrived, he had decided to help us."

"Bennigan didn't want his help," Mayflower said. "And he and his men handled Elliston."

"But if it comes to it, who's going to handle Bennigan?" she asked.

"Well," Mayflower said, "that's what we hired Temple for, and he's an experienced lawman."

"I'm worried," she said. "There's just too much tension."

"Well," Mayflower said, "maybe I should have a talk with Temple and get some idea of what's going on."

"That sounds like a good idea."

"Did he go back to his office?"

"I don't know."

Mayflower stood up.

"I'll go and have a look. He keeps long hours."

"Be careful, Dad."

"I will," Mayflower said. "You just stay inside."

***

Temple went back to his office and told Campbell to go and get some food.

"Then come right back. We have to talk."

"Yessir."

As Campbell opened the door to leave, he practically ran into Mayflower's burly chest.

"Mr. Mayflower's here, Sheriff."

Campbell tipped his hat to the man and slid past him. Mayflower entered and closed the door.

"What brings you here, Mr. Mayflower?" Temple asked.

"May I sit?"

"Of course."

Mayflower sat in a chair across from Temple and wondered how to start?

Chapter Thirty-Two

"Patty tells me you had supper with Captain Bennigan," Mayflower said.

"That's true," Temple said. "He invited me over."

"What was on his mind?"

Temple sat back in his chair, wondering how much he should tell the president of the town council.

"All right, here it is," Temple said. "He wanted to warn me that eventually he would stop holding his men in check."

"And then what?"

"And then they would rob the bank, for a start," Temple said. "After that they'd go to work on the town."

"So young Charlie was right about what they did to that last town."

"If Bennigan's telling me the truth."

"Why would he lie about a thing like that?"

"Why would he warn me?"

"Did you ask him that?"

"I did," Temple said. "He said he wanted to give me a fair chance at stopping them."

"Do you think he was on the level?" Mayflower asked. "Maybe he's just trying to spook you."

"No, I think he was on the level," Temple said.

"So what do you intend to do?"

"I'm calling in my deputies, and we'll talk about it," Temple said. "If we watch his men closely, we might be able to toss a few of them into a cell before Bennigan gives them the go ahead."

"And then what?"

"And then we'll have to see how many we can kill before they kill us."

"Is that a joke?" Mayflower asked.

"I wish it was," Temple said. "There's one other possibility."

"And what's that?"

"He seems to feel that everything is a game."

"So you think he's just playing a game with you?"

"I said it's a possibility."

"I don't know," Mayflower said. "In my dealings with him, Bennigan doesn't strike me as that kind. He comes off as very serious."

"So then you believe him."

"I do," Mayflower said. "I think you need more deputies."

"I had enough trouble hiring these two," Temple said. "They're young."

"Then maybe we should send for Clint Adams," Mayflower said.

"Do you think he'd come?"

"I think if Patty asked him to."

"Do you know where he is right now?"

"No," Mayflower said. "We'd have to send out some telegrams, and hope that Bennigan leaves the telegraph alone."

"I think with me having only these two young deputies, that sounds like a good idea," Temple said.

"I'll have Patty get on it," Mayflower said. "There's no telling how long it would take, even if we find him."

"We'll just hope for the best," Temple said. "Meanwhile, I'll do what I can to keep the lid on."

"How do you think you can do that?"

"I think if Bennigan likes games," Temple said. "I might be able to play one with him. I just need to keep him occupied until I can think of something."

"I wish you luck," Mayflower said.

Mayflower started for the door, then turned back, a thoughtful look on his face.

"I might be able to come up with a few men who can handle a gun."

"I need gun hands," Temple said, "not hunters."

Mayflower nodded and left.

***

"What makes you think Clint would come back here if I ask him?" Patty asked her father.

They were sitting in his office, across his desk from each other.

"My dear daughter, do you think I didn't know what kind of relationship you two had?"

"Dad—"

"Never mind," Mayflower said, "you're a big girl. Right now we need to get those telegrams out."

"To where?" she asked.

"When he left here he rode south," Mayflower said. "Let's cover the south and hope he didn't get very far."

"How do we do that?"

"We'll leave it to Lyall at the telegraph office," Mayflower said. "You just need to write it, and he'll send it out."

"But what do I say?"

"It's very simple," Mayflower said. " 'Help!' "

Chapter Thirty-Three

Clint had traveled mostly on horseback, but when he wanted to give the Tobiano a rest, he went by rail. He managed to cover 500 miles, which put him in Denver.

He was sitting at a poker table in the back room of Dusty's Casino when he saw his friend, private investigator Talbot Roper walk in. Roper wasn't a poker player, so it was fairly obvious what he was doing there.

"Deal by me, this time," he said, rising.

He met Roper at the bar which had been erected for the game.

"What brings you here?" he asked. "I know it's not poker."

"Do you know anybody in Warbend, Montana?" Roper asked.

"I do," Clint replied. "Why?"

Roper took a telegram from his pocket and handed it to his friend. Clint unfolded it and read it. It had been sent a few days before.

"Help!?" Roper asked. "Somebody knows you very well."

Clint folded the telegram back up and put it in his pocket.

"Have you ever heard of Bennigan's Rangers?"

"A bunch of self-styled fake lawmen," Roper said. "They wear badges they made themselves."

"I should've known you'd know them."

"You have some dealings with them?"

"No," Clint said, "but it looks like I might."

"What's it about?"

"Let me cash out of the game and I'll tell you about it . . .

***

Clint and Roper left the back room to go to the main bar, and Clint explained.

"You sound guilty for leaving," Roper said, when Clint finished.

"I tried my best not to get involved," Clint said. "And when Bennigan got there he made it clear he didn't need or want my help."

"So you left town after they did the job?"

"Right."

"I don't think you need to feel guilty about any-thing," Roper said.

"Maybe not," Clint said, "but there was other infor-mation about those rangers that indicates they might not leave that town standing."

"It wasn't up to you to live there until something happened," Roper said.

"Maybe not . . ."

"You're going, aren't you?"

Clint nodded.

"You against . . . how many?"

"Bennigan's got a dozen men."

"What's the law like there?"

"I don't know," Clint said. "When I left, they were looking for a sheriff."

"Jesus, Clint," Roper said, "you're riding into a hornet's nest."

"Probably."

"You want some help?"

"I can't ask you to do that," Clint said.

"You're not asking," Roper said, "I'm offering. I've got nothing to do, right now. I might as well keep you from getting killed."

"I appreciate it."

"Besides" Roper said, "you might have some more help sitting at that table, in there."

***

In Warbend there was an indication that things might be going bad.

Mayflower walked into the lobby of the hotel and joined his daughter at the desk.

"What is it, Dad?" Patty asked, reading the expression on his face.

"We're not going to hear back from Clint," he said. "The telegraph is out."

"Bennigan?" she asked.

"It's likely, but we can't prove it."

"I remember what happened when Elliston's men tore the poles down," she said. "This could be the beginning. Should you tell the sheriff?"

As Temple entered the hotel Mayflower said, "I have a feeling he knows."

The lawman joined them at the desk.

"I sent one of my deputies out to check the poles," he said. "They're down."

"Could they have fallen over on their own?" Mayflower asked, hopefully.

"Not a chance," Temple said. "They were pulled down."

"So this is the start," Mayflower said. "Have you managed to jail any of Bennigan's men?"

"Not a chance," Temple said. "They're all keeping to the letter of the law."

"Do you think this is the signal Bennigan was talking about?" Mayflower asked.

"Maybe," Temple said, "but I think the signal will be a lot louder."

The sound of shots came from outside.

"You mean like that?" Mayflower asked.

"Both of you stay inside," Temple said, and headed for the door.

Chapter Thirty-Four

When Temple got to the street people were running towards him. His deputies were in the middle of the street, looking around. When they saw him they ran over, too.

"Where were those shots from?" Temple asked.

"The bank, Sheriff. We were just getting ready to go over there," Tyler said.

"Okay, let's go."

The three lawmen ran to the bank in time to see three men coming out the front door. There were several other men standing out front.

"Those are Bennigan's men," Campbell yelled.

"This is it, then," Temple said. He drew his gun, and then the deputies followed.

"Hold it!" Temple shouted to Bennigan's men.

There were six of them, and they began to fire. Several slugs hit Deputy Tyler, putting him down immediately.

"Take cover!" Temple shouted to Campbell, but it was too late. A bullet hit the young deputy in the chest, and he hit the ground.

Temple took cover behind a buckboard that was on the street. While he watched, another man came out of the bank. It was Bennigan, himself.

"Hold your fire!" he shouted, and his men stopped firing. "Sheriff? You can come out, my men won't fire."

Temple wondered what Bennigan's game was now? They had just killed his two deputies. Why not him?

"Come on, Sheriff," Bennigan said. "We have some business."

Temple stood straight and stepped out. Bennigan was right in front of the bank, with his men around him.

"So this is the beginning?" he called out.

"The beginning for us," Bennigan said. "The end for you and your deputies."

"And what about the town?"

"Well, once you're gone, we'll just take what we want."

"Where am I going?"

"You're not riding out, if that's what you think," Bennigan said. "Put that gun back in your holster, and I'll give you a chance."

Temple holstered his gun. Bennigan stepped down into the street.

"So how do we do this?" Temple asked.

"Just you and me," Bennigan said.

"And if I kill you?" Temple asked. "Your men gun me down?"

"Don't worry about that, Sheriff," Bennigan said. "You can't kill me."

Temple knew this was the end. He had a chance to finish Bennigan, but then his men would kill him. Maybe, if he could kill the Rangers captain, the rest of the men would leave town.

"Okay, Bennigan," he said, "whenever you're ready."

"The first move is yours, Sheriff."

***

After Temple ran from the hotel Patty and her father, instead of obeying and remaining inside, ran out the front door. They saw people frantic in the street, and the three lawman going the other way. They followed until they came within sight of the bank, where they stopped to watch. They saw the two deputies go down, then heard what Bennigan said to Temple.

"What's he going to do?" Patty asked.

"What can he do?" Mayflower replied, as Temple stepped out into the open.

"Oh, no," Patty said.

"If he can kill Bennigan—" Mayflower said, but he stopped when Temple drew.

***

The sheriff drew his weapon as fast as he could, but he wasn't fast enough. Bennigan drew and fired first. The bullet hit Temple in the right shoulder, and he dropped his gun. He went down to one knee, covering the wound in his right shoulder with his left hand.

Bennigan walked across the street and stood in front of Temple, looking down at him.

"It's too bad, Sheriff," Bennigan said. "My guess was you were a good man in your time."

"I don't understand," Temple said. "Why put this group together to stop outlaw gangs, and then turn outlaw yourselves?"

"I told you before, Sheriff," Bennigan said. "It's all a game." He pointed his gun at the kneeling man. "And you lose."

He pulled the trigger.

***

"Oh my God!" Patty said and covered her face with both hands. "He shot him in cold blood." She looked at her father. "What now?"

"Now?" he asked. "Now we're in trouble."

Chapter Thirty-Five

For the next week Bennigan and his men owned the town. They took what they wanted from stores, from whores, from hotels and saloons. They had killed Sparks when they robbed the bank, but after killing the sheriff and his deputies, they didn't kill anyone else.

Bennigan and his men continued to occupy rooms in the Mayflower Hotel, and to eat in the dining room. Patty had no choice but to continue to feed them.

On this morning, a week after Temple was killed, she finished serving them, and when they left the dining room she went to her father's office.

"Are they gone?" Mayflower asked.

"Fed and gone. Some of them went to their rooms, others left the hotel." She sat. "I don't know how much longer I can just treat them like guests. They're killers, worse than Elliston and his men."

"The mayor and I are looking for a new sheriff now," Mayflower said, "but the telegraph is still out."

"How long before they decide to just kill us all and burn the town?" she wondered out loud.

"Who knows?" Mayflower said.

***

Clint reined his horse in as they came within sight of the town. The two men with him did the same.

"What is it?" Roper asked.

"Look at it," Clint said. "It looks like a ghost town."

"It sure does," Roper said. "Empty streets. Just some damaged wagons in the dirt."

"Bennigan and his men must be having their way with the town," Clint said.

"How many did you say?" the third man asked.

"Bennigan and twelve men," Clint said.

"Worse than four-to-one odds." Roper said.

"So what do we do?" the third man asked.

"We'll ride in behind the Mayflower Hotel," Clint said, "enter through the back door. We need to talk to Mayflower and his daughter."

"Lead the way," Roper said.

Clint started toward the town with his two friends following behind.

***

They reined in behind the hotel and dismounted. Clint went to the rear door, found it unlocked, and led the way in. They walked down a hall until they reached the door of Mayflower's office. He opened the door and the three of them went in rapidly.

Mayflower stood up from his desk, then recognized Clint.

"Oh my God," he said, grabbing Clint's hand and pumping it. "You got Patty's telegram."

"Yes," Clint said, "it got to me in Denver. I was playing poker, but when I read it, I started out right away. These two friends of mine offered to come along. This is Talbot Roper."

"Mr. Roper," Mayflower shook his hand.

"And this man was playing poker with me. When he heard where I was going and why, he offered to come along. Meet Bat Masterson."

"My lord," Mayflower said, shaking Bat's hand, "this is a pleasure."

"I didn't really volunteer," Bat said, "but what the hell. I couldn't let Clint and Roper face thirteen men themselves."

"But there's still only three of you," Mayflower said. "The sheriff had two deputies, and they're all dead."

"How did that happen?" Clint asked. "Tell us everything . . ."

***

After Mayflower finished his tale Clint, Roper and Bat exchanged glances.

"The sheriff and his deputies were shot down on the street," Clint said. "We won't give them that chance."

"What will you do?" Mayflower asked.

"Come up with a plan," Clint said. "Meanwhile, we'll need a place to stay, and some food. We've ridden a long way in a short time."

"Bennigan and his men are all in this hotel," Mayflower said. "Since Elliston and his men were in the Palace, it's been empty."

"Good," Clint said. "We'll stay there."

"What about our horses?" Roper asked.

"We'll put them in Bruiser's livery," Clint said. "He'll keep them hidden."

"You can get into the Palace from the back," Mayflower said. "I'll have Patty bring you some food. She'll be very happy to see you."

"Where are all the people?" Bat asked.

"They've been staying off the street since the bank was robbed and our lawmen were killed," Mayflower said.

"Smart," Roper commented.

"It's getting dark," Mayflower said, "you should be able to get around without being seen. Patty'll be right there with some supper."

"Some of that beef stew she makes should be enough," Clint said.

"I'll tell her." Mayflower put his hand on Clint's shoulder. "Thanks for coming back, Clint."

"Let's hope we can do something," Clint said.

Chapter Thirty-Six

When Clint, Roper and Bat entered the deserted Palace Hotel they each took a room on the second floor. They had a bed, a table and some chairs. There were some chests of drawers, but they were in pieces.

The three men gathered in Clint's room. They had already left their horses with Bruiser, who was also happy to see Clint back.

"We can't light any lamps," Clint said. "We'll have to get some candles."

"I could use a drink," Bat said.

"Patty's bringing food," Clint said. "If I know her, she'll also bring something to drink."

"How do you want to handle this, Clint?" Roper asked.

"I'm not sure," Clint said. "Bennigan's got a dozen men, but maybe we can simply take him out."

"And the rest would run?" Bat asked.

"We can hope."

They had kept the door to the room open so Patty could find them.

"Clint?" she called, from the hall.

"In here."

She came running into the room and threw her arms around him.

"I'm so glad to see you," she cried.

She looked around, saw Roper and Bat, then stepped back, looking embarrassed.

"Patty Mayflower, meet Talbot Roper and Bat Masterson.

"I'm so glad you're all here. I have some food and things out back—candles, and whiskey.

"We'll go get it," Bat said, and he and Roper left.

"It's been horrible here, Clint, horrible. I watched Bennigan shoot Sheriff Temple in cold blood."

"We'll see what we can do, Patty," Clint said. "I hope it's enough."

"B-but you, and Bat Masterson—"

"—and Roper," he said. "But there's still only three of us."

Bat and Roper returned, carrying the provisions.

"The stew should still be hot," Patty said, taking the pot. "I brought some bowls, and candles since you won't be able to light the lamps."

Clint lit one candle while she spooned the stew into bowls.

"This should be enough," he said, setting the candle on the table.

"Sit down and eat," Patty said, putting the bowls and spoons down.

Clint, Roper and Bat sat and started to eat.

"Wow, this is wonderful," Roper said.

"Thank you," Patty said. "Here's something to drink." She put a bottle of whiskey on the table.

Bat grabbed the whiskey, took a swig, then passed it to Roper, who did the same and passed it to Clint.

"You all need food and rest," Patty said, "and you can do something tomorrow."

"We'll make a plan," Clint said. "You better get back to the Mayflower, Patty. We don't want Bennigan and his men to wonder where you are."

"They'll want to eat," Patty said. "I'll have to feed them, and act normal, if I can."

"Does Bennigan eat with his men?"

"Yes."

"We could take them while they're eating," Bat suggested.

Clint looked at Patty.

"Do they all eat at the same time?" he asked.

"Not every night," she said. "Some of them spend time in the whorehouse, or in a saloon."

"We could take them there, first," Clint said. "A few in the whorehouse, a few in a saloon. Then the rest of them eating in the Mayflower."

"Do they have their guns while they're eating?" Roper asked Patty.

"Yes," she said, "they're all armed all the time."

"Well," Clint said. "We can't do anything tonight, but you get back there and act normal. We'll come up with a plan."

"All right," she said. "I'm so glad to see you all."

She hurried from the room.

"That's a pretty girl," Roper said.

"And a brave one," Clint said.

"And a helluva cook," Bat said, helping himself to more stew.

"It sounds like we can avoid facing all the men at the same time," Roper said.

"Yes, but we'll have to know when they're in the whorehouse, or a saloon, and how many are still in the hotel."

"We need a bird dog," Bat said. "Somebody to keep an eye out."

Clint thought of young Charlie and said, "I think I have just the man—or boy."

They continued eating and passing the whiskey bottle until it was empty, and they were full.

"We need some sleep," Clint said. "You two go to bed and I'll take the first watch, just to be safe."

Roper and Bat each took their own candle and went to their rooms.

There were a couple of sips left at the bottom of the whiskey bottle, so Clint finished them off, reviewing the plan in his head. It made sense to split the men up and take them by surprise. And, according to what Patty told them, it seemed as if those men were splitting themselves up.

Clint cleaned his guns until it was time to wake Roper for the next watch. The one thing they had to make sure of was that they weren't taken by surprise.

Chapter Thirty-Seven

In the morning Patty appeared with a pot of coffee and some bacon.

"This was all I could put together," she said. "I have to get back to make breakfast for those animals."

"That's okay," Clint said. "We appreciate this."

She kissed Clint quickly on the cheek and rushed back to the Mayflower.

"That girl's got a lot of spunk," Bat said, chewing on some bacon.

"She sure does," Roper agreed.

"Okay," Clint said, "I've been thinking about this, and it seems to me since Bennigan's men are splitting themselves into groups, all we have to know is when they're there."

"And you said a boy could help with that," Roper said.

"Why would he?" Bat asked. "This is dangerous."

"Charlie's got a big crush on Patty," Clint said. "He'll do whatever she asks."

"And if he gets killed, she'll feel all the guilt," Roper pointed out.

"He's not going to get killed," Clint said. "We're not asking him to face anyone. Just let us know where the men are."

"The whorehouse is a good bet," Bat said. "We'd be catching them with their pants down."

"And then the saloon," Roper said. "They're bound to be drunk."

"Bennigan's too smart to be caught himself in either place," Clint pointed out. "He's going to have to be last."

"This might take a few days, but once we hit the whorehouse, they're going to know we're here," Bat said.

"They'll know somebody's here," Clint said, "but they won't know it's us."

"When do we get started?" Bat asked.

"Next time Patty comes over here, we'll have her talk to Charlie," Clint said. "In fact, she can bring the boy over here for us to talk to."

"So we're going to be in here at least another day," Bat said, reaching into his vest pocket. "Good thing I brought some tools." He brandished a brand new deck of cards. "Shall I crack these?"

***

Roper was not a poker player, but to pass the time he agreed to play. They had nothing to play for, and neither Clint nor Bat wanted to take Roper's money, so they played for nothing but bragging rights.

At one point Roper threw in his hand and said, "God, I'm glad we're not playing for money."

"If we did it would be a good lesson for you," Bat offered.

"Never mind," Roper said.

Patty arrived with some lunch, even though Clint had told her she didn't need to bother.

"It's just sandwiches and a pale of beer," she said, "but I'll bring something better for supper."

"I'll tell you what you could bring us," Clint said.

"Name it," she asked.

"Not it," Clint said, "who? I need you to bring Charlie back here."

"What do you want with Charlie?"

"We need someone to let us know when some of Bennigan's men are in the whorehouse, or a saloon. We're going to try and take them while they're split into groups."

"Is it dangerous?" she asked. "He's just a boy."

"He rode out to find Bennigan's Rangers. That was more dangerous. Now we just want him to watch."

"All right," she said. "I'll bring him with supper."

"Good."

She left and they unwrapped the sandwiches and began eating, washing them down with beer.

"I'm going to get spoiled with this treatment," Bat said.

"So am I," Roper said.

"Let's try not to," Clint said. "Hopefully, tomorrow we can start taking these Rangers apart."

"After we eat," Bat said, "right?"

***

That evening Patty arrived with roast chicken, a bottle of brandy . . . and Charlie.

"Hello, Mr. Adams," the boy said. "Patty says you need me."

"Charlie," Clint said, "this is Talbot Roper, and this is Bat Masterson."

"Bat Masterson? Really?" Charlie asked. "Wow."

Clint turned to Patty. "You should get back."

"Right." She took some of the dishes they were finished with and headed back to the hotel.

"What do you need me to do?" Charlie asked.

"We know that some of Bennigan's men go to the whorehouse, others to a saloon. We need to know when they go, and how many."

"I get it," Charlie said. "You wanna catch 'em with their pants down."

"Smart boy," Bat said.

Charlie looked proud.

Chapter Thirty-Eight

They ate their supper, played some more poker, and then went to their own rooms for the night. Clint took first watch, again. Charlie's instructions were to come running when he had the information they needed. But nothing would probably happen until late the next day.

He woke Roper in four hours for the next watch, and turned in, extinguishing his small candle.

He wasn't asleep long when something woke him. As he sat up he saw Patty sneaking into his room.

"Patty," he said, "you took a chance coming here. Roper's on watch. He might have shot you."

She smiled as she lit the small hunk of candle.

"Mr. Roper saw me coming down the hall," she told him. "He knows I'm here."

"Why *are* you here, Patty?" he asked.

"I think you know," she said, coming toward the bed. "I've missed you. I'm so glad you're back."

"Patty—"

She unbuttoned her shirt and peeled it off. There was nothing underneath, so her breasts burst forward toward him. She sat on the edge of the bed to remove her boots, then stood and slid out of her trousers. When she was completely naked, she climbed onto the bed with him. She unbuttoned Clint's skivvies and peeled them off him, so that they were both naked.

"We'll have to be quiet," Clint whispered to her.

"I told you, Mr. Roper knows I'm here. And I don't think it would be a surprise to Mr. Masterson."

"Maybe not," Clint said, "but we don't want anyone else hearing us."

"Oh, I see," she said, running her fingers over his bare chest. "All right, we'll be quiet."

She slid her hand down his body so that she could grasp his hard cock. She caressed his penis and testicles until he was good and hard, then shimmied down to take him into her mouth. She sucked him avidly, wetly, making it as difficult as she could for him to keep quiet.

When he couldn't take it anymore, he reached for her and pulled her up on top of him. She quickly moved her hips until the tip of him was pressing against her pussy . . . and then she took him inside with a quick thrust.

The heat of her enveloped him, and she started riding him up and down. He found her rhythm, matched it, and they moved that way together until he couldn't take it anymore, and exploded into her . . .

***

They laid together for a while, catching their breath, and then he said, "Patty, you have to go."

"But your friends know I'm here."

"That doesn't mean I want to rub it in their faces," he explained.

"Oh, all right," she said, sliding from the bed. He watched by the light of the candle while she dressed.

"We don't want your father catching on either, do we?" he asked.

She giggled and said, "Dad already told me he knew."

"And he didn't mind?"

"He said I'm a big girl."

She pulled on her boots and stood up.

"I'll be back in the morning with some breakfast," she said.

"Don't bother with lunch," Clint said. "If things go according to plan, we might not be here."

"Wouldn't that be true for supper?" she asked.

"Some of the men might go to the whorehouse in the afternoon," Clint said. "But you're right. We might catch some of them in the saloon at suppertime."

"I'll bring it anyway, just in case."

By the time she slipped from the room, Bat was on watch. He stuck his head out the door and she smiled at him and waved.

***

They woke in the morning, hoping that this would be the day they could get something done.

"Once we take a few of them in the whorehouse, and then the saloon, Bennigan will know something's up," Clint said.

"But he won't know who it is," Roper said.

"He's bound to keep the rest of his men together," Clint said. "In the end we may have to face seven or eight of them."

"That's better than thirteen," Roper said.

Bat looked up from a game of solitaire and replied, "You said it."

When Patty arrived with coffee and bacon she seemed a bit embarrassed.

"Thanks for this, Patty, but remember, stay away the rest of the day."

"How will I know what's happening?" she asked.

"I'll have Charlie tell you," Clint said.

"That's good," she said. "He can also tell me if I should bring you supper."

"Patty—"

"Good luck," she said, and rushed out.

Chapter Thirty-Nine

At breakfast Sergeant Sharkey ate with Captain Bennigan while the other men occupied three different tables.

"What's the plan for today, Cap'n?" Sharkey asked.

"We've taken the bank," Bennigan said, "cleaned out the general store and some of the other shops. I think we might be done here in the next few days."

"Then we can leave and burn it?"

"I don't see why not."

"The men will be glad to hear that," Sharkey said.

"What are they doing today?" Bennigan asked.

"A few of them will go to the whorehouse this afternoon, as usual," Sharkey said. "They haven't yet used up all the whores."

"That's what they're for," Bennigan said.

"What about you and Miss Mayflower?" Sharkey asked.

"I'll be taking care of her before we leave," Bennigan said.

"Some of the other men will be in the High Card Saloon. They're just about ready to take it apart."

"That's fine with me," Bennigan said. "I've got our next job picked out."

"How'd you do that with the telegraph out?"

"I chose it before that," Bennigan said. "It's a town in Wyoming."

"I like Wyoming," Sharkey said.

"What are you going to be doing today, Sharkey?" Bennigan asked.

"Me? I just might take a walk around town, to see what hasn't been picked clean." he laughed.

"Good," Bennigan said. "You'll let me know. Get that kid over here, I want more coffee."

***

Charlie was helping Patty serve Bennigan's Rangers their breakfast and was keeping his ears open.

"Hey, kid!" Sharkey yelled. "More coffee over here."

"Yessir."

Charlie went over and filled their cups.

"Hey, kid," Bennigan said. "I'm real glad you brought us here. This town's been good to us."

"Yessir."

"Don't feel bad about it, though," Bennigan said. "When we leave, maybe we'll take you with us? You want to be a ranger?"

"That sounds good, Sir," Charlie said.

"Yeah, you bet it does," Bennigan said.

Charlie backed off and went into the kitchen.

"There's a table of three out there that's talkin' about goin' to the whorehouse, this afternoon," he told Patty.

"You've got to tell Clint."

"Not until I know exactly when they're goin'," Charlie said.

"All right, good thinking."

"I sure hope Mr. Adams and Bat Masterson can handle the Rangers," Charlie said. "Captain Bennigan just said he might take me with 'em when they leave, and make a Ranger out of me."

"Omigod!" Patty said. "Charlie, you wouldn't—"

"No, Patty," he said. "I'd never want that. But if he takes me—"

"We won't let that happen, Charlie," Patty said. "Clint and his friends won't let it."

"I hope you're right."

"Let's get finished here and then we'll tell my father what's going to happen."

***

Charlie stayed around the hotel lobby so he'd know when the men went to the whorehouse.

"Hey, kid."

He turned and saw the three men coming toward him. One of them threw his arm around the boy.

"You ever had a whore?" he asked. His name was Stevens.

"What? W-well, uh, no—"

"You wanna come along with us?" the man asked. "We'll getcha one. Make a man outta ya."

The three men laughed as Charlie blushed. Patty came into the lobby and saw what was happening.

"Leave him alone!" she snapped. She came over and pulled Charlie away from them.

"Oh, I get it," Stevens said. "You want the boy for yerself, don't ya, girlie."

"You're disgusting!" Patty said.

"You bet we are!" Stevens said. The three men went out the front door, laughing and slapping each other on the back.

"All right, Charlie," Patty said. "You better go and tell Clint."

"Right."

"And make sure nobody spots you."

"I'll go the back way," the boy promised, and ran down the hall to the back.

Chapter Forty

Charlie rushed to the Palace Hotel and went in the back door. He ran up to the second floor to Clint's room, where he found all three men.

"It's happenin', Mr. Adams," he said. "Three men have gone to the whorehouse."

"Okay," Clint said. "You get back to the Mayflower."

"Yes, Sir."

Charlie ran from the room.

"Ready?" Clint asked.

"We've been ready since we got here," Bat said.

"I don't think we'll need rifles for this maneuver," Clint said. "Pistols will do."

He led the way from the room, down the stairs and out the back door.

"Where's the whorehouse?" Bat asked.

"West end of town," Clint said.

They turned that way and started to run. The streets were empty, so they didn't bother staying off the main street. When they reached the whorehouse they saw a two-story, gaudy yellow building.

"Jesus, this place stands out," Bat said.

"How do you want to play this?" Roper asked.

"Let's go to the front door and talk to somebody," Clint said. "See where the three men went."

They went to the front, climbed the steps and knocked. The door was opened by a full-bodied redhead, wearing a very filmy nightgown underneath a robe.

"Gentlemen," she said, with a big smile, "welcome to Lulu's Whorehouse. Are you interested in blondes, brunettes . . . or me?" she asked.

"Are you Lulu?" Clint asked.

"I am. This is my establishment."

"Lulu, three men came here just before we did. They're Captain Bennigan's men."

Her expression suddenly changed.'

"Those three? Are you with them?"

"No," Clint said. "We're here to free the town of Bennigan's Rangers, starting with those three."

"It's about time," she said, pulling her robe tightly around her.

"Now, where did they go?" Clint asked.

"They each have a regular girl," Lulu said. "Right now they're upstairs, in their rooms."

"And what rooms are they?"

"Rooms five, seven and eight. The girls are Grace, Enid and Debra. And if you can take those men out of here before they start beating on my girls, I'd appreciate it."

"That's exactly what we intend to do, Lulu," Clint said.

As they stepped past her, she looked Roper up and down.

"You're a handsome one," she said. "After you finish with those men, why don't you come back?"

"Thanks for the invitation," Roper said.

"No charge?"

Roper smiled and said, "I'll try."

She addressed all three of them.

"You gents can go on upstairs. Do what you've got to do, but take care of my girls."

"We will," Clint said.

The three of them went up the stairs as quietly as they could.

"I'll take room five, Roper you take seven and Bat, you take eight,"

"Let's do it," Bat said.

They moved along the hall, each stopping in front of their assigned door.

Clint put his left hand on the doorknob, his right on his gun, and nodded to Roper and Bat. They all opened the door at the same time.

As Clint entered he saw a tall, skinny, naked man on a bed with a hefty blonde girl. She screamed and covered her bulky body with the sheet.

The man, who had been on top of the girl, looked over his shoulder and said, "Get outta here."

"Sorry," Clint said, "but I'm giving the orders. Get off the girl."

The man moved over her and stood. He looked over at his gun, on a chair nearby.

"Go ahead and try it," Clint said.

"Who are you—wait a minute. I know you," the man said. "You're Adams, the Gunsmith."

"That's right."

"B-but, you left town."

Clint smiled and said, "I'm back."

***

As Bat stepped into his room, he saw the naked back of a long, lean brunette as she was riding the man beneath her. When she turned to look over her shoulder, he saw that she already had a black eye.

"You can get off him, sweetie," he told her. "He's done."

"Thank God!" she said, hopping off the man. She grabbed her robe to cover herself.

"You can go," Bat said.

"Thank you."

The portly man on the bed sat up and stared at Bat.

"What the hell—" he said. He turned his head to look at his gun, across the room.

"You'll never make it," Bat said. "Just get up and get dressed."

"You're crazy," the man said. "Do you know who we are?"

"I do," Bat said. "Let me introduce myself. William Barkley Masterson, at your service."

The man's eyes went wide.

"Bat Masterson?" he asked.

"That's right," Bat said. "Still want to try for that gun?"

"No, Sir."

"Then get dressed."

"Yes, Sir."

The man started pulling his pants up, hopping on one leg, and then the other.

***

Roper opened his door and stepped in. A burly man was slapping a small, naked girl. He turned and said, "Whoever you are, get outta here before I kill you."

Roper pointed his gun at the man. He didn't want to fire unless he had to.

"Step away from the girl."

"Who, this girl?" the man asked. "Is she yours? She's my usual whore, but if you want her—"

"Just stop talking," Roper said, "and get dressed." Roper looked at the girl. "Put on your robe and get out if here."

The girl did what she was told, but stopped right next to Roper before leaving.

"Thanks, Mister."

She fled from the room.

The burly man stood up. His body was covered with coarse, black hair.

"You know who you're dealin' with?" he demanded. "I'm one of Bennigan's Rangers."

"Not anymore you're not," Roper said. "You're headed for a jail cell."

The man laughed.

"Ain't no lawmen in this town."

"Maybe not," Roper said, "but there's a jail, and that's where you're headed. Of course, if you'd rather die—"

"Hey, no, no," the man said. "Relax. We can talk about this."

"Get dressed, and we'll talk about it," Roper said, "in jail."

Chapter Forty-One

All of the whores in Lulu's were happy to see the three Bennigan's Rangers marched out of the house.

Outside, Roper said, "I saw a jail house on the way here. There may not be any law, but we could still use the cells."

"Good idea," Clint said, "Let's go."

"Look, Adams—" Clint's man started.

"Adams," the burly man said. "He left town."

"He's back," the tall, skinny man said.

The portly man said, "And this is Bat Masterson."

"What's goin' on here?" the burly man demanded.

"Your days of running rough shod over this town are over," Clint said.

"Wait til the Captain hears about this," the skinny man said.

"When he hears about it," Clint said, "it'll be from me. Now move!"

They walked the three men to the jail. The street was still empty, so they got there without attracting too much attention. Everything was covered with dust, but there were three cells and the keys were on the wall.

Clint grabbed the keys and marched each man into a cell.

"We won't be here long, you know," the portly man said. "Our men will come looking."

"He's right," Bat said. "We can't just put them in these cells. They'll start yelling the minute we leave."

"Bat's right," Roper said. "We better bind and gag them."

"Good idea," Clint said. "You two stay here with them. I'll go to the livery for some ropes and gags."

"Right," Bat said.

Roper pointed his gun at the three men and said, "They'll keep quiet until you get back."

Clint left the jail.

***

Bruiser brought Clint some ropes and gags.

"Here you go, Mr. Adams," he said. "You got three of 'em, huh?"

"So far," Clint said. "There'll be more before we're done."

"You gonna kill 'em?"

"We're going to take them as quietly as we can, so we don't attract the others until we're ready for them."

"Sounds like a helluva plan to me."

Chapter Forty-Two

Clint returned to the jail. He, Roper and Bat tied and gagged the three Bennigan men.

"All right," Bat said, looking down at the three hog-tied prisoners. "Now what?"

"The saloon," Clint said. "We'll wait for Charlie to let us know Bennigan's men have gone there."

"We won't be able to take them as quietly as we did these," Roper said.

"Then once we take them, we'll have to be ready for the rest," Clint said. "For now, let's get back to the hotel so Charlie can find us."

"What about them?" Roper said, indicating the hog-tied men.

"Nobody knows they're here," Clint said, "and they're not going to get free."

"We could just kill them," Bat said.

"You want to gun down three helpless men?" Clint asked. "Go ahead."

"Yeah, okay," Bat said. "Leave them trussed up."

"Then let's get back to the hotel," Roper said.

"Maybe Patty will bring us some food," Bat said, hopefully.

***

When they reached the Palace Hotel there was no sign of Patty, or Charlie.

"Do we have any food left?" Bat asked.

"No," Clint said, "just half a bottle of brandy."

"That'll have to do."

They sat and passed the bottle around.

"Okay," Roper said, "step one is accomplished. Now we need step two, the saloon."

"First we have to find out which saloon they're in," Clint said, "and how many of them there are."

"And that's up to young Charlie," Bat pointed out.

"We might have a few hours," Clint said. "Even if they head for a saloon now it'll take a while for them to get good and drunk."

Bat shook the brandy bottle and said, "One thing's sure, we aren't getting drunk."

"All we can do is wait," Clint said.

Bat set the bottle down on the table, and took out his deck of cards.

"Poker?" he asked.

***

In the end, Bat played solitaire while Clint and Roper watched. When they heard somebody in the hall Bat put the cards down and they all watched the door. Charlie came running in.

"They're in the saloon, Mr. Adams," he said.

"How many of them?"

"Four."

"Which saloon?"

"The High Card."

"How long have they been there?" Bat asked.

"About an hour," Charlie said. "I couldn't get away before now."

"All right, Charlie," Clint said. "You go back. Stay with Patty."

"Yessir."

Charlie ran out.

"All right," Clint said, looking at Bat and Roper, "Step two."

***

They got to the High Card Saloon without encountering anyone on the street. From inside the saloon came loud voices and some music. Clint moved to a window and looked inside.

"How many people are in there?" Roper asked.

"More than four," Clint said. "And some others, including the bartender and piano player. There are also some girls."

Roper looked around at the empty street.

"Looks like nobody else is coming," he said.

"How do we know which four are Bennigan's men?" Bat asked.

"One of you will have to go inside and find out," Clint said.

"That'd be me," Roper said. "Somebody might recognize Bat."

"All right," Clint said, "we'll watch and listen from out here. At the first sign of trouble, we'll come in."

"Right," Roper said.

He went through the batwing doors. Clint and Bat moved to the windows on either side.

***

Roper entered the saloon and went to the bar.

"Beer," he said to the bartender.

"Comin' up."

As the bartender put a beer down in front of him, Roper said, "I heard Bennigan's men spend time in here."

"You don't wanna deal with them," the bartender said. "Most of my customers stay away because of them."

"Looks like you got a few here," Roper said.

"Sometimes they let a few in to drink and celebrate."

"Celebrate what?"

"They never know," the bartender said. "They just want company."

"And the girls?"

"They always want girls."

"Okay," Roper said, sipping his beer, "which ones are they?"

"Why's it matter to you?" the bartender asked.

"We're going to take them out," Roper said. "Cut down the odds."

"You and who else?"

"You'll see," Roper said. "Just point them out."

"Two in the back near the piano, and two in front."

"That's good enough," Roper said. "Now get ready to duck."

He turned to look at the four men. Each pair had a girl sitting with them.

"I heard there are some of Bennigan's men in here," he said loud enough for everyone to hear.

The Piano player stopped, and the Bennigan men looked at him.

Chapter Forty-Three

"What's it to you?" one of the men asked from the back table.

"I just wanted to see what a bunch of cowards look like," Roper said.

"You've got a big mouth, friend," one of the men from the front table said.

"You think so?" Roper asked. "Why don't you show me?"

The four men stood up, and the two girls hurried away from their table. The piano player also ran for cover, as did the other patrons.

"You're gonna find out," one of them said.

"That's good," Roper said, "but first I'd like you to meet my friends." As the batwing doors opened, Roper continued, "Bat Masterson, and Clint Adams, also known as the Gunsmith."

The bartender ducked down behind the bar.

The four men looked at Clint and Bat.

"The Gunsmith?" one of them said. "You left town."

"I came back, and I brought friends," Clint said. "You men want to show us how good you are?"

The four men looked back and forth at each other.

"Come on," Clint said. "One of you has to be a spokesman. Call the play.

"Against you?" one of them said.

"What's your name?" Clint asked.

"I'm Jenkins."

"Well, Jenkins," Clint asked. "what's the play going to be here?"

Clint knew if they had to fire it would alert the rest of the Rangers.

"Are you going to draw?"

"Against you?" Jenkins said. "Not a chance."

"And the rest of you?"

They all shook their heads.

"All right, then," Clint said. "Take your guns out with two fingers and drop them. Come on, all four of you."

"You won't get away with this," Jenkins said. "You'll still be outnumbered."

"Not by as much as you think," Bat said. "Now drop 'em."

All four obeyed, drawing their pistols from their holsters and dropping them to the floor.

"Now what?" Jenkins asked.

"Now we're taking a walk to the jailhouse," Clint said.

As they started walking the men out of the saloon the bartender stood up.

"If anyone comes looking for these men," Clint said to him, "you haven't seen them."

"Whatever you say, Mr. Adams."

"Make sure the rest of these people stick to the same story."

"Don't worry," the bartender said. "They will. We're all real glad you're here."

Clint followed the others out.

***

When they got to the jailhouse they hogtied and gagged the four men and put them into the cells with the other three.

"You can't get away with this," Jenkins said.

"I think you'll see that we can," Clint said, gagging the man. He finished securing Jenkins and stepped out of the cell. With all three cells locked, he left the cell block.

"Now what?" Roper asked.

"We've got seven down," Clint said, "That leaves six to go, including Bennigan. They should all be in the Mayflower, or we would have heard from Charlie again."

"Charlie might be back at the Palace, waiting for us," Bat said.

"You're right," Clint said. "Let's get back over there. Even if these seven get free of the ropes, they can't get out of the cells." Clint looked at the keys in his hand. "We'll keep these with us."

"That oughta keep them here, no matter what," Bat said.

"Let's get back to the hotel."

***

When they got to the Palace they found it empty.

"Without word from Charlie about the others, what do we do?" Roper asked.

"We're going to have to go over there and hope we find the rest of them," Clint said, "including Bennigan."

"We'll have to shoot it out with them," Bat said, "at two-to-one odds. We don't have much choice."

Chapter Forty-Four

"We'll take our rifles, in case we don't make it to the Mayflower before they see us," Clint said.

"Okay," Roper said.

They all picked up their rifles and checked them. They were just about ready to go when they heard somebody in the hall. In moments Patty came running in.

"Where's Charlie?" Clint asked.

"They're not letting him leave," she said. "They're . . . playing with him. I'm afraid they're going to hurt him."

"How many of them are in the Mayflower?"

"I don't know, exactly," she said. "Five or six."

"Five, then," Clint said, "That's all that's left."

"You-you've killed the others?"

"We've put them out of action," Clint said. "Where's Bennigan?"

"He's in the Mayflower, watching his men toy with Charlie."

"If they have Charlie and we go over there, they'll use him against us," Bat said.

"Yes, they will," Clint said. "We'll have to get him away from them."

"How will you do that?" Patty asked.

"We won't," Clint said, "You will."

***

Patty entered the Mayflower and went right to the dining room. She saw that Bennigan was still sitting there, watching his men laughing, and pushing and pulling Charlie from pillar to post.

She went right up to Bennigan and said, "If you want supper for you and your men I'll need Charlie."

"Is that a fact?" he asked.

"It is," she said. "Tell your men to leave him alone."

"I'll tell you what," Bennigan said. "If you want them to leave Charlie alone, you have to agree that after supper, you'll come to my room."

"What?"

He reached out and touched her cheek.

"I'm tired of waitin', sweetie."

"You can't mean—"

"Or maybe I'll just have them kill 'im."

"No!"

"Then do you agree?"

She slumped her shoulders, hoping that Clint would be able to keep her from this promise.

"I agree," she said.

"Sharkey!"

The sergeant came over.

"Tell the men to leave Charlie be, and sit. It's almost suppertime."

"Yessir." He turned to the men. "Let him be!"

Immediately, the men stopped pushing Charlie back and forth.

Patty ran over and grabbed the boy.

"I need you in the kitchen."

"Yes, Ma'am."

She dragged Charlie to the kitchen, then turned to him and said, "Go and open the backdoor. Hurry!"

He ran out the kitchen door that led to a hallway to the backdoor. When he opened it Clint held his finger to his lips. Bat and Roper were right behind him.

"Go back to the kitchen and stay there with Patty."

Charlie nodded and hurried back.

Clint turned to Bat and Roper and said, "Back around to the front. Let's get them in a crossfire. I'll count to twenty before I step in."

"Right."

They turned and ran to the front.

Clint crept down the hall to the kitchen, where Patty and Charlie were standing to one side. Clint reached twenty in his count when he got to the kitchen door.

Then he stepped through.

Chapter Forty-Five

Bennigan spotted Clint as soon as he stepped from the kitchen. Before he could say or do anything, both Bat and Roper stepped in from the lobby.

"Shut up!" he shouted to his men. The noisy crew settled down, looked at their boss, then looked around.

"Clint Adams," Bennigan said. "I thought you left town."

"I did," Clint said, "some time ago. But I'm back."

"And you brought help," Bennigan said.

"Yes," Clint said, "these are my friends, Bat Masterson and Talbot Roper."

"I've heard of both men," Bennigan said. "But you're still a little outnumbered."

"Not by much," Clint said. "You'll notice you're missing about seven men."

"Sharkey," Bennigan said, "where are Jenkins and the rest?"

"The whorehouse," Sharkey said, "and the High Card Saloon."

"They were there," Clint said, "but not anymore."

"Are they dead?" Bennigan asked.

"No, but they're out of commission. All you've got left is what's in this room."

"We still outnumber you," Bennigan said.

"We've been outnumbered before," Clint said.

Clint's gun was in his holster, but Bat and Roper were holding theirs.

"It's your call, Bennigan," Clint said.

"Yes," Bennigan said, "it is. Take 'em!"

Bennigan's men all stood, knocking their chairs and tables over, and drew their guns. Bat and Roper began firing. Clint drew his gun and fired.

Roper and Bat darted to one side. Some of Bennigan's men went down, others ducked behind the fallen tables and fired back. Clint saw that Bennigan took cover. Some of Bennigan's men might've been behind tables, but they were caught in a crossfire. Before long, they were all done, and the firing stopped.

"Bennigan?" Clint called. "Are you still alive?"

"I'm here."

"You might as well stand up and toss your gun."

"Sharkey!" Bennigan shouted. "Sharkey!"

"He's dead, Bennigan," Clint said. "All your men are dead or locked up. It's only you, now."

"Then let's make it you and me, Adams," Bennigan called back. "I gave Elliston and Sheriff Temple a fair chance. That's all I want from you."

Bat and Roper stood up.

"Your call, Clint," Bat said.

"Yeah, okay," Clint said, not only to Bat and Roper, but to Bennigan. "Stand up, Captain."

Bennigan stood up from behind his overturned table and holstered his gun.

"This should be interesting," Bennigan said. "Nobody's ever beat me before."

"Then it's your play," Clint said.

"I don't usually draw first, but—" Bennigan reached for his pistol, but Clint outdrew him cleanly and fired once. The bullet punched a hole in Bennigan's chest. He staggered, looked down at himself, then at Clint and said, "That was fast!" before he dropped his gun and fell over.

Roper and Bat walked among the fallen men, while Clint checked Bennigan.

"He's dead," he said.

"So are they," Bat said.

Patty and Charlie came from the kitchen, while Mayflower came running from his office.

"What the hell—" he said, looking around.

"That was amazing!" Charlie said. "I never saw anythin' so fast."

"It's all over, Dad," Patty said. "Captain Bennigan is dead."

"And his men?"

"They're all dead," Clint said. "The rest are in jail cells."

"How did you manage that?" Mayflower asked.

"We took them out a few at a time," Clint said. "There are seven in the cells at the jail."

"So it's all over?" Mayflower asked.

"It is," Clint said.

"I'll let the mayor know," Mayflower said. "We'll get a new sheriff assigned to handle those men."

"Then I guess Bat and I can get moving," Roper said.

"Oh, no," Patty said, "not before you get a good night's sleep here, and a decent meal."

"She's right," Clint said. "Stay one night and get some rest."

"And you?" Bat asked.

"I'll be leaving in the morning, too," Clint said.

"This town owes you gents a big send-off," Mayflower said.

"One of Patty's fine meals will be enough," Clint said.

"If it's anything like the meals she's been bring up at the Palace," Bat said, "I agree."

Mayflower said, "I'll get some men in here to clean up, and then go and talk to the mayor."

"Meanwhile," Patty said, "I'll clean three rooms for you gentlemen, and then get busy preparing a fine meal."

As the Mayflowers left to see to their tasks, Bat said to Clint," I think that girl's going to try and make it hard for you to leave, Clint."

"She will be able to make it difficult," Clint said, "but I think I've had my fill of Warbend."